WEEKLY READER
Children's Book Club
Education Center • Columbus 16, Ohio

PRESENTS

THE SECRET OF CROSSBONE HILL

BY WILSON GAGE

By the same author

SECRET OF THE INDIAN MOUND

The Secret of

WILSON GAGE

Crossbone Hill

ILLUSTRATED BY *Mary Stevens*

THE WORLD PUBLISHING COMPANY

CLEVELAND AND NEW YORK

PUBLISHED BY The World Publishing Company
2231 West 110th Street, Cleveland 2, Ohio

PUBLISHED SIMULTANEOUSLY IN CANADA BY
Nelson, Foster & Scott Ltd.

Library of Congress Catalog Card Number: 59-5920

FIRST EDITION

WEEKLY READER
Children's Book Club
Edition, 1960

THE SECRET OF CROSSBONE HILL

Chapter 1

"GOSH, HOW MUCH LONGER does this causeway go on?" asked David Vance.

"We'll be there in about half an hour," his father answered.

"Can't you go any faster?" Kathy wanted to know.

"Kathy, will you please sit down and stop snuffling down the back of my neck?" cried Mr. Vance.

"I was *not* snuffling," said Kathy with dignity, but she settled back on the seat and looked out the window. The car slowly rattled on across the wooden causeway. On each side the tall green marsh reeds and grasses rippled away endlessly.

A kingfisher swooped suddenly across the road. "Oh, a kingfisher!" cried Mrs. Vance.

David suppressed a sigh. They had only seen about a hundred and two kingfishers in the last hour, and every time one had flashed into view his mother had cried, "Oh, a kingfisher!"

The kingfishers were as monotonous as the rest of the landscape. Half the morning the car had moved down a sandy, rutted road with tall pines on either side, each tree just exactly like the others. And then they had come to the causeway, a rutted wood-and-sand roadbed rising up out of the surrounding marsh, over which the car had to travel even more slowly. For half an hour they had crept through the salt marsh, with David and Kathy growing more and more impatient with every passing minute.

"Over there is the swamp," Mr. Vance said, waving his hand toward the left, where a dim line of trees made a smudge along the horizon. "This is the marsh. People around here are very careful to make the distinction. If there are trees and water, it's swamp. Just reeds and grass and mud and water— that's the marsh."

David stored this piece of information away for future reference.

Up ahead loomed a lone big cypress tree. Gray tassels of moss streamed from its limbs and swayed in the wind. The car inched toward it.

Kathy leaned over to David. "If you ask me, we're lost!" she announced in a loud whisper. "We've passed that selfsame tree six times now. We're just going around and around in a circle. We'll just go around and around till we run out of gas, and then we'll sit on the side of the road waiting for help to come."

"Oh, turn blue, will you, Kath?" David said in exasperation.

Kathy's big brown eyes opened wider than ever. "You wait. You'll see. We'll get hungrier and hungrier and we'll try to catch a kingfisher and eat him, only we won't be able to and we'll have to stew the seat covers and eat them."

"Kathy, you should have eaten more breakfast if you're so hungry now," said Mrs. Vance.

"Oh, I'm not hungry," cried Kathy, leaning forward again. "I'm too excited to be hungry. Will we

13

be there soon? Can we go in swimming right away? Do you think there are any sharks?"

"Hundreds of them," answered Mr. Vance. "Now do sit back and try to be patient. It isn't so much longer now."

David looked around eagerly. How could his father tell? There wasn't anything different to see. The causeway stretched far ahead into the marsh. On David's left the scattering of cypresses and moss-hung live oaks was coming a little closer to the causeway.

"You sure would have a long walk in case your car broke down or something like that," he said.

"What a cheerful outlook you have, David," exclaimed Mr. Vance. "Ah! There it is!"

"There what is?" asked Mrs. Vance.

"That hill," said Mr. Vance, pointing to a dark hump on the horizon. "The house is very near now."

"That's a hill?" queried David. "Some hill!"

Mr. Vance laughed. "Well, it's the nearest thing to a hill around here," he stated. "I understand it's seventy-four and a half feet above sea level. We'll climb it some day if you think you can stand the rarefied atmosphere."

David grinned. "I'll let it go," he said. "Just bring on that old ocean; that's what I want."

The causeway came to an abrupt end. A short distance ahead of them the road divided, one branch running north through a jungly tangle of trees and vines, and the other south along the edge of the marsh.

"The north road leads to Digby. We go south," Mr. Vance said, "and it's less than a quarter mile."

He slowed the car to make the turn, and Mrs. Vance gave a gasp. "Oh, look, look, look!" she cried.

"Not more kingfishers," thought David, and turned his head. And even he drew in his breath in surprise.

For there in the shallow water at the marsh's edge stood a flock of enormous long-legged white birds. When Mr. Vance stopped, the birds did not seem to mind the car. One or two stretched their supple necks and turned their yellow bills toward the intruders, but the rest ignored them. Motionless on their slender black legs, they stood among the green-and-yellow reeds with the sun gleaming on their backs.

"What are they, Mother?" whispered Kathy.

15

"American egrets," Mrs. Vance whispered back.

"Gosh, they're taller than I am," Kathy said. "Will they bite?"

"Oh, aren't they beautiful!" Mrs. Vance exclaimed. "Fourteen of them!"

"Fifteen," corrected David, pointing.

The fifteenth bird came skimming over the tops of the grasses, trailing its black feet behind it. It circled slowly and then with a graceful gesture of its wings, it slowed, thrust down its legs, and lit among the others. Folding its wings, it too stood silent and still.

"Jeepers," said David, "I liked the way he banked and lowered his landing gear and all."

"Judith, this is high tide," Mr. Vance told his wife. "I expect at low tide this place will be alive with all sorts of birds."

"Oh, I'm looking forward to it," Mrs. Vance said blissfully.

"Well, I'm looking forward to the ocean," said David hurriedly. There was no point in letting his mother get started on birds now. They'd be here the rest of the day if she did. "I'm hot."

Mr. Vance started the car forward.

"Me too," chimed in Kathy. "I'm sizzling, bubbling, boiling. Hurry, Daddy, hurry!" She began to bounce up and down on the seat.

"What? And have you miss one of the most exciting, the most startling, stupendous, thrilling sights in the whole low country of South Carolina," Mr. Vance exclaimed. "A sight seldom witnessed before in the annals of history!"

17

"What? What?" asked David.

"Why, this truly amazing and remarkable hill," said Mr. Vance. "Observe its noble proportions and its air of grandeur."

"Oh, Daddy, come on!" urged Kathy.

But as the car rolled by, David studied the hill with interest. It certainly looked strange and somehow mysterious, rising up out of the flat land like an Egyptian pyramid. He made a mental note to explore it someday soon.

"There's a house," cried Kathy. She leaned for-

ward over her mother's shoulder. Is that one it?"

"The trail's end," answered her father.

The house was set on wooden piles, a precaution against the floodwaters of storms and hurricanes. It was smaller than David had expected. It had weathered to a silvery gray color and looked slightly crooked, as though it had been almost blown off its underpinnings by a strong wind and nobody had

bothered to straighten it up again. Along one side it had what Kathy called a "ruffle of bushes" of some sort, with sandy-looking leaves and odd-shaped berries.

Mr. Vance pulled up under a small tree at the back steps and turned and grinned at Kathy. "Now if you'll slip into that gorgeous new bathing suit of yours, I'll conduct you personally to the ocean," he said.

"Not till we get the car unloaded," commanded Mrs. Vance, opening the car door.

David scooted out and up the back steps with the key his father had given him. He opened the door and stepped in. This was the kitchen and it was tiny, but next to it was a huge living room. Beyond was a bathroom and two small bedrooms. It was dim and stuffy in the house, with the shutters over the windows, and it smelled rather queer—a combination of salt and dust and fish with a suspicion of stale suntan lotion.

But the four rooms looked wonderful to David. The paintless chairs and tables, the sagging beds, the woven mats—raveling a little at each end—

on the floor, the kerosene lamps, all spelled freedom from worry and care. No more watching out where you put your feet or wet towels, no more trying to remember to keep your smudgy hands off the wood-work. For two months it wasn't going to matter if he tracked mud into the living room.

Kathy picked out her room, and David took the other one cheerfully. In the living room Mr. Vance showed David how the couch opened out with a screeching wail to make a big double bed. "Mother and I will sleep here," he said. "And if you hear this thing folding up in the night, kindly rescue us before it's too late."

Then the last of the suitcases were brought in, and there was a wild scramble for bathing suits.

"I'm sure I packed mine," groaned Kathy. "I remember I put it right on top."

"That was before you decided to bring your doll collection," Mrs. Vance reminded her. "You had to repack everything then, remember?"

"But I *couldn't* have left out my suit!" exclaimed Kathy tearfully. "Oh, here it is, in my bathrobe pocket."

21

"Just the place I would have looked first," teased Mr. Vance.

At last they were all dressed, and Mrs. Vance had rubbed suntan oil all over them. "You've hardly *seen* the sun since last September," she told David.

He wiggled away and ran out through the screened front porch and down the steps after his father.

There was a wooden walkway a block long across a stretch of rough sand, shells, and coarse grass. David rushed ahead, jumping off the end of the walk and running over the hot, slippery dry sand. A moment later he was lying on his back under the blue sky, letting the waves lift him gently up and float him softly down while the cool water rippled around his ears and chin.

Wasn't it lucky that Daddy had to come to South Carolina to get the material he needed for his magazine articles and that a friend had this cottage to lend them for two months? And it was certainly lucky Daddy had decided to bring the whole family. David had had to do a lot of hard studying on Saturdays and after school each day, taking tests and doing extra papers, so he could leave two weeks before school closed.

But it was worth it, he thought, spitting out a mouthful of salty water. Think of his class, listening to Miss James talking about adverbs, and smelling green beans because it was Thursday and the cafeteria always had green beans on Thursday. While here he was happily swimming at the beach.

He began to tread water, looking out at the horizon. Africa was out there and his father looked as though he'd traveled half the distance. Mr. Vance's head was just a tiny dark spot.

David turned toward the shore. Kathy was paddling about in the shallow water, and his mother was swimming out toward him.

"Isn't this wonderful?" she asked him. "I feel like a new woman already. What new woman shall I be —Madame Curie? Or Cleopatra?"

"Never mind being somebody famous—just be a good cook, will you?" said David.

Mrs. Vance made a face at him and they headed for the beach. Mr. Vance came splashing back and they all agreed it was time for lunch. They started for the house.

"Look," said Kathy. "You can see that hill wherever you go."

"I expect you can see it a good way out at sea too," Mr. Vance said. "It's probably man-made. This country here used to be a great plantation, with rice fields all around. Some plantation owner may have built that hill as a signal post for ships bringing him goods and coming to take his rice away to England. Or he may just have had a Nebuchadnezzar complex."

"Like the Hanging Gardens," David explained to Kathy.

"I know, stupid!" said his sister witheringly.

"Maybe the Indians built it," suggested Mrs. Vance.

"I don't think so," replied Mr. Vance. "It's called Crossbone Hill, and to my mind that's a corruption of some French name, like Grosse Pointe, and that would mean a Huguenot landowner."

"Crossbone!" cried Kathy. "Oh, Daddy, like the Jolly Roger! Pirates, Daddy. I bet the pirates lurked out there in the ocean and waited for the merchant ships to come sailing in. And one of the pirates would stay here on shore, and when the ship was tied up at the plantation wharf he'd go to Crossbone Hill and light a big fire, and the pirate ship would come swooping down on the merchant ship with broadside after broadside, and at it they'd go!"

Her father stared at her. "Kathy, you should go far in this world," he said at last. "You have what's known as a fertile imagination and an inexhaustible supply of words. Exhausting to me, but inexhaustible to you, apparently."

"Were there any pirates around here, Daddy?" asked David.

"Oh, yes," Mr. Vance answered. "In the early seventeen hundreds the pirates gave the planters quite a lot of trouble. Why, Blackbeard himself was captured near this coast."

"You see!" cried Kathy triumphantly. "It *was* pirates who built Crossbone Hill. I bet they buried treasure around here somewhere, and I'm going to find it!"

Chapter 2

WHEN DAVID WOKE, the first thing he heard was the sea. Just the faraway crash of the waves, not the whisper of the water running back and forth across the sand. But enough to let him know that here he was, at the beach, hundreds of miles from home and American history and multiplication of fractions.

He stretched his legs till his feet stuck out from under the covers. He could smell bacon and coffee, so he knew his parents were up. He drew in his feet and snuggled down in the hollow of the mattress.

Suddenly he bounced out of bed. He was at the *ocean*. What was he doing lying around when he could be out exploring? He dressed in a rush, getting his arm through the neck of his T-shirt and having to start all over, knocking over a chair, and generally getting himself flustered. When he finally burst into the kitchen he was red in the face and out of breath.

His father set down his coffee cup and gave him a surprised look. "Ah, it's only you," said Mr. Vance. "I had discounted elephants and migrating herds of caribou. In fact, I had just told myself that I was the sole witness to the birth of a new volcano in the room next to me. I'm somewhat disappointed."

"I was in a hurry," apologized David, sitting down at his place at the table where a glass of orange juice waited for him. He drank it fast, trying not to gulp. His father handed him a plate with bacon, eggs, and a cinnamon bun on it.

"Where's Mother?" asked David.

"Out on the walkway with her field glasses," his father answered. "Or do I hear her coming in now?"

"Are the children up?" called Mrs. Vance. "Kath, you slug-a-bed! Get dressed and come to breakfast."

In a minute Mrs. Vance appeared in the kitchen door. She was dressed in blue jeans and a white shirt;

28

her cheeks were flushed pink, and her hair blown by the wind.

"Gosh, Mother," cried David, "you look so young and pretty!"

Mr. and Mrs. Vance both began to laugh. "The salt air does wonders, even for decrepit old crones of thirty-four," Mr. Vance teased.

"Well, thank you for your kind words anyway, David," said his mother. She had a pair of binoculars around her neck and another pair over her shoulder. Under her arm she carried a small blue book, a fat brown book, and a huge green one. "And guess what I saw in the marsh?"

"What?" asked David dutifully.

"A ruddy turnstone!" cried Mrs. Vance.

"I can't believe it," Mr. Vance said, astonished.

"Really I did, Phil," Mrs. Vance said earnestly. "I watched it a long time through my glasses."

"Oh, if there is such a thing, I don't doubt you saw it," said Mr. Vance. "It's just hard for me to believe in a creature with such a name. Ruddy turnstone! You might as well tell me you saw a healthy logroller."

Mrs. Vance giggled. "Here's a picture," she said,

holding out one of her books. "Isn't he fascinating? He's really an arctic bird, just on his way through."

"No doubt a short wait between trains," Mr. Vance explained to David, taking the book. "Say, he's quite a bird. And that really is his name."

David craned his neck to see the picture. He had to admit that the stocky bird, with its red back and white front and a curious spidery pattern of jet-black over its head and throat, was a most intriguing creature.

"Neat," he commented. Birds at the ocean were a big improvement on the little gray-and-yellow warblers his mother was always talking about at home.

"Then you don't mind if I watch them," his mother said, smiling.

David turned red and drank his milk. The truth was, he did mind at home. He didn't like having the other guys ask him why his mother was always wearing those binoculars and staring around at the treetops. And once his mother had dropped a lemon meringue pie smack on the floor, before anybody had even had a taste of it, because she said a Baltimore oriole had looked in the window at her.

But the worst thing happened at a PTA meeting

last year when David's own class was giving a program on music for the mothers. Two girls were just about to play "The Marine Hymn" on their recorders when Mrs. Vance stood up and said loudly, "There's an evening grosbeak in that pine tree."

Several of the mothers screamed; one of the little girls had burst into tears; and some teachers went to fetch the janitor because they thought it was some kind of burglar in the pine tree. Everybody laughed about it later, that is, everybody except David. He wished his mother would take up knitting or first-aid classes or something like everybody else's mother did.

But here at the beach it was different. He didn't mind so much.

Mr. Vance stood up as Kathy came in. "Hello and goodbye, Miss Vance," her father said. "You'll have to arise a mite earlier than this if you expect to see your poor old father in the mornings. I have a good long drive to the library, you know. In other words, I've got to go."

"Oh, Daddy, I thought you'd stay here today," Kathy cried.

"Alas, no, my Princess," Mr. Vance answered. "I

cannot stay with you. A wicked magician has put a spell upon me, and every day at this time I must vanish into thin air in order to make a living."

"Oh, noble Prince," said Kathy seriously, "how can I free you from this evil enchantment?"

"By boiling seventeen toads and eating them with a sauce of grasshoppers," Mr. Vance answered.

"Ugh!" Kathy shuddered. "You'll just have to stay enchanted."

"Heartless wretch," Mr. Vance cried and went out to collect his notebooks and pencils.

"Eat your breakfast, Kath," Mrs. Vance instructed. "Then you and David make your beds before you go out on the beach."

David stared at his mother. "You mean I have to make up that saggy, baggy old cot?" he asked.

"That's what I mean," answered his mother firmly.

David hurried to his room and jerked the rough sheets up over the lumpy mattress. He hung his pajamas on a convenient chair back and made a stack of his dirty clothes and a damp towel in the middle of his dresser.

He sprinted out the front door and down the

steps. His bare feet thudded over the wooden board-walk, and then he was running on the hard-packed sand of the beach.

David had been to the ocean once before, but that was two years ago and in a very different setting.

There had been long stretches of tidy white sand, with tall palm trees and red-roofed cottages crowded close to the shore. And on the beach, no shells, no busy sandpipers, nothing but an occasional empty cigarette package or beer can.

33

But this—this was different. He might as well be on a desert island, he thought, standing there with the wind streaming around his ears and the creamy froth of waves foaming around his feet. He could barely see the house. It had disappeared into the tall sea oats and scraggly myrtles that covered the rough sandy shore.

There were birds everywhere, running and swooping and diving. And this beach was quite littered with shells. David turned his back to the ocean and searched along the tide line. The first thing he saw was a starfish, bright-red and orange, feebly waving its many feet in the air.

David stared at it. He was almost positive starfish couldn't bite or sting or do anything painful.

"Dave! Dave!" someone called. "Wait for me!" It was Kathy running toward him, holding a bottle of suntan oil in one hand. "Mother says rub some of this on."

"Oh, holy cats!" complained David. But he rubbed the oil over his face and arms anyway. The sun was pretty hot, and he'd hate to get a bad burn now and miss something.

"Look here," he said, pointing at the starfish.

34

Kathy squealed and jumped back away from it.

"Oh, for Pete's sake, he can't bite," David told her. A little gingerly he picked the creature up. For a minute he considered putting it down Kathy's back. But there had been a sort of gentleman's agreement between him and his father that on this trip he wouldn't tease Kath more than he absolutely had to.

"It's alive!" shrieked Kathy. "Oh, throw it back, throw it back, David!"

"All right, all right," he answered. "Don't get excited."

He raised his arm and flung the starfish as far as he could. For a minute it floated on the surface of a green wave, and then it vanished in a flurry of foam. Kathy let out her breath in a long sigh.

"We saved its life," she said proudly. "David, I tell you what let's do. Let's walk up and down the beach and every time we find a poor little fish or oyster or starfish that's been thrown up on the sand, we'll throw it back in and save its life. It'll be a good work, almost like being missionaries."

"You're crazy," said David. "Most of the things you threw in would come floating back again."

35

"Well, all right," Kathy agreed. "Besides, I wouldn't like touching oysters. They're so slimy."

"They have shells over the slimy part," David pointed out.

"Oh, yes"—Kathy nodded—"I forgot. Do you suppose that's an oyster shell? Oh, isn't it pretty?"

She picked up a small pink cockleshell and held it out for him to see.

"Look at the yellow ones," David pointed out. In a few minutes they had a handful of delicately colored shells in all shapes and sizes.

"I could make a bracelet out of these," Kathy announced, holding up some tiny lavender and purple ones.

"Now, that's an idea," said David enthusiastically. "We might get a lot of shells and make jewelry out of them and then sell them. I sure would like to earn some money this summer. I wanted to buy Mother a super birthday present next month, but then I had to pay for my bike tire, and now I'm broke."

"There's Mother now," said Kathy. They ran back down the beach, and Kathy presented her mother with the collection of shells.

"They are lovely," Mrs. Vance told her. "Oh, oh, what's that?"

She snatched up her binoculars and stared at the sky. "It's a tern," she breathed. "Quick, David, get that blue book and look up terns!"

David picked up the blue book and leafed back and forth through it. "Hurry, hurry!" cried Mrs. Vance. "It's a big one. It must be a Caspian tern."

David found the place. "Black cap, large red bill, and forked tail," he read. "The bill of the Royal tern is slenderer, orange rather than red."

"Does that bill look orange or red to you?" asked Mrs. Vance.

Kathy peered at the big white bird which hovered over them as though it was as interested in Mrs. Vance as she was in it. "It looks sort of orangish-red to me," said Kathy. "Or maybe reddish-orange."

The bird threw back its bill, uttered a derisive "Gowk!" and flew off.

"David," asked Mrs. Vance, "does a Caspian tern say 'Gowk'?"

"He says 'Kaah,'" David read helpfully.

"Well, what about a Royal?" Mrs. Vance wanted to know.

"Nope, he says 'Keer,'" David told her.

Mrs. Vance sighed. "Well, at least I've got two months to solve the puzzle. I do believe that's a willet up there." She began to walk up the beach.

"Let's get some more shells," suggested David.

"She sells sea shells along the sea-shell shore," sang Kathy. "Oh, Mother forgot her blue bird-book."

"It doesn't matter; she's got the brown one with her," David said. "I'll put the blue one here on the boardwalk, and we'll get it when we go home."

"All right," said Kathy. And then as they walked down to the water's edge, she went on, "But, Dave, you know what I think? I think it would be better to look for pirate treasure than to try to make jewelry and sell it."

"Aw, Kath, you've got rocks in your head," rejoined David. "There's no pirate treasure around here. And even if there was, you don't know where to look for it."

"There is too treasure," Kathy insisted. "And anyway, I'd a heap rather look for treasure than sit around making jewelry. And who would buy it? We're the only people around here."

David was trying hard to think of a possible

39

market when Kathy spied a sand dollar. By the time they had each found several of these pretty objects and crammed the pockets of their shorts with shells, they had walked a good way.

"Let's go back," suggested Kathy. "I'm hot and thirsty."

David agreed and they turned around. When they got to the boardwalk, Mrs. Vance was waiting for them. "Come along," she called. "We've just got time for a swim before lunch."

David and Kathy ran. They were sprinting up the wooden walk when suddenly David stopped. "Did you get your book?" he asked his mother. "I left it on the walk."

"I didn't see it," said Mrs. Vance. "Run get it for me."

David turned back. The boards felt hot and splintery under his feet. He reached the end of the walk, but he didn't see the book. He looked all around carefully. He stepped off the walk, got down, and peered under the planks. A lizard skittered away in the sand. But there was no blue book.

His mother came and stood beside him. "Can't you find it?" she asked.

"No'm," he answered disconsolately. "I laid it right here. You can ask Kath. But now it's gone, and I can't see where it's got to."

Mrs. Vance glanced up and down the sand on each side of the walk. "I do hope it's not lost," she said sadly.

"If it's lost, I'll buy you a new one," promised David. Boy, he'd have to sell a million bracelets made of shells now.

"Oh, Dave," cried Mrs. Vance. "I couldn't ever replace it. It had all my notes about warblers in it—things I'll never be able to remember."

Slowly they walked back along the hot boards. David knew his mother must be thinking that he'd put it down carelessly and lost it. But he hadn't. He'd laid it down right there on the walkway.

But what had happened to it? Because what Kathy had said was true. There wasn't anybody there but them.

Chapter 3

DAVID SPENT a very gloomy afternoon. He knew his mother thought he had carelessly lost the book; he knew he hadn't. But what had happened to it? As Mr. Vance said when he came home, it was hardly likely that a small blue guide to birds had flown off by itself.

Kathy giggled. "Maybe a crab took it away," she said. "Dave and I saw some awful big ones this morning."

She and her father and brother stood at the end of the boardwalk, ". . . revisiting the scene of the crime," David said dolefully.

"Or maybe a lady pelican went off with it," Mr.

Vance added. "Even now she is at home instructing her children in the differences between the blue-tailed whippersnapper and the russet-voiced wing-ding. Dave, are you sure you left the book right here?"

"He really did, Daddy," Kathy piped up. "I saw him. And we went walking down the beach and didn't come back till we saw Mother standing there. Not either of us."

"And you didn't see anybody on the beach at all?" asked Mr. Vance.

David shook his head. "We weren't looking for anybody," he added. "Who else would be here?"

"Well," answered Mr. Vance, "there's a house back in the swamp somewhere, not far from the end of the causeway. It's supposed to be deserted, but this morning I saw smoke rising up from that direction. Maybe some old tramp or beachcomber is staying there, and he found the book and appropriated it."

"Well, I hope so," said Kathy. "It seems so sort of ghostly for a book to go off by itself. It gives me the gruesome shivers."

"Either way, I guess the book's gone," David mourned.

"I wouldn't leave anything else lying around unless I was going to keep an eye on it," Mr. Vance warned. "Don't look so downcast, David. Nobody blames you. Somehow this is the very last place I'd expect to find a sneak thief."

By the time he went to bed David was slightly more cheerful. He still regretted that he hadn't run after his mother with the book that morning, however. He knew she had owned the guide for a long time. It was full of notes she had made, and of course she would never be able to replace those, no matter how many new copies of the book she might buy. He was still thinking about it when he fell asleep.

In fact, he dreamed about it. First he dreamed he was chasing a huge crab which was carrying the book in its claws. He chased it right down the middle of the main street at home, but a policeman stopped him and cried, "Why aren't you doing your homework?"

David turned around to go back and start on his arithmetic when his mother came running up. "Did you find my book?" she asked. David shook his head. "Well, you'll just have to stand in this pan of hot water until you do!" she cried.

44

Meekly, David stepped in. The water grew hotter and hotter, and his feet began to burn. David danced up and down until the pan turned over, but still his feet burned and smarted.

"David!" said his mother's voice in his ear, and he struggled up out of his sleep. "Whuzzer matter?" he asked sleepily. "Something wrong?"

His mother smiled. "That's what I came to ask you," she told him, holding up a kerosene lamp. "You were moaning in your sleep, and I thought maybe you were feeling bad."

"No," David answered. "It was my feet. I dreamed that I was standing in hot water and burning my feet. Say, they really do hurt. What's the matter with them?"

He poked two red swollen objects out from under the covers.

"Oh, David," gasped Mrs. Vance. "Your poor feet! They're sunburned! Didn't you rub any suntan lotion on them?"

"Gosh, no," David exclaimed. "I never thought about it. Ow, they're roasted all right."

"Oh, David, it's my fault. I should have told you. And Kathy too. I'm so sorry," Mrs. Vance sympa-

thized. "Wait here and I'll get something for that."
She was back in a minute with a jar of some kind
of salve that was cool and white. She spread it gently
over the tops of his feet and then arranged his sheets
so the weight of the covers didn't press on them.
"There," she said.

"Thanks, Mother," he said sleepily. Already his
feet felt better.

46

There was a sudden wail from the next room. "My feet!" moaned Kathy. "Oh, my poor feet. I've been poisoned! My feet have been poisoned!"

David couldn't help laughing. Depend on Kathy to think up something like that. His mother hurried away, and David drifted off to sleep.

The next morning the tops of his feet were blistered and the bottoms tender and sore from walking on the hot dry sand. He could barely hobble. He limped into the kitchen and was surprised to find his father there, reading a book while he drank his coffee.

"I thought you'd be gone," commented David.

"So did I," replied Mr. Vance. "But the gods decreed otherwise. I had a flat tire and my spare's in such bad shape I was afraid to drive to the library on it. I'll drive up to Digby this afternoon and get the tire fixed. I've got some work I can do here this morning, organizing notes and things like that."

"I'll be glad to help," said Mrs. Vance, handing David his plate.

"Thanks, I'll take you up on that," Mr. Vance told her. "Here comes the second wounded veteran."

Kathy did not walk in. She slid in on the seat of

47

her shorts, with her legs extended straight in front of her.

"You'll get splinters," warned Mr. Vance.

"Well, I just can't walk," sighed Kathy.

"Me neither," grumbled David. "I meant to climb that hill today and do lots of exploring, but I guess I won't now."

Mr. Vance looked despairing. "Why is it that every time circumstances force me to work at home, everybody else in this family has some ailment that keeps him in the house and underfoot?"

"I didn't get sunburned on purpose," sniffed Kathy.

Mr. Vance laughed. "I know you didn't, Kath," he said. "Let me see now—What entertainment can I arrange for my two invalids?" He looked thoughtful, and then suddenly he snapped his fingers. "I've got it! Quick, Mother, the thermos bottle."

"Right here," answered Mrs. Vance. "And I can whip up some Vienna sausage sandwiches in just a minute. What's your plan?"

"There's a boat that goes with the house, you know," Mr. Vance explained. "No, Kathy, not a yacht, just a plain flat-bottomed rowboat. It's used for crabbing and shrimping in the marsh. Now Mother will pack your lunch, I'll drive you to the causeway, and you can explore the marsh in the boat."

"Oh, Phil, is that safe?" asked Mrs. Vance.

"Safe as houses," he answered. "I used to do it all the time when I was younger than Kathy. Dave knows how to handle a rowboat. Even at high tide the water's not waist-deep, and both these hoodlums can swim. And the boat's on the north side of the causeway, so there's no outlet to the sea."

"They'll get lost," protested Mrs. Vance.

"Not as long as they can see Crossbone Hill they won't," answered Mr. Vance.

David watched the worried frown on his mother's face. Sometimes he wished she wouldn't be so cautious and careful. "I've got a compass," David said to reassure her. He was eager to try it. Exploring a marsh all by himself, without any grownups around! Neat!

Of course there'd be Kathy, but Kathy wasn't too bad, as far as sisters went. He knew a lot of guys with ten-year-old sisters, and he wouldn't swap with any of them. Kath might be a little brainless, but

49

she wasn't prissy or a tattletale or anything awful like that.

The preparations didn't take long. Even while Mrs. Vance was arguing she was making the sandwiches and filling the thermos bottle. It wasn't quite ten o'clock by the time Kathy and David were settled in the boat.

"Now, Kath, no jumping around," warned Mr. Vance. "Dave, have you got your watch? The tide turns at twelve nineteen, so start back before two thirty. Otherwise you'll get stuck and have to wade in."

"All right," David agreed.

"And be careful," put in Mrs. Vance.

"Jeepers, Mother, I'm eleven years and seven months old," protested David. "Don't you think I've got any sense?"

Mrs. Vance laughed. "I suppose so," she said. "It's just hard for me to realize you're growing up."

Mr. Vance gave the boat a shove, and it wobbled out into the water. It was maneuvered with a pole, not oars, David had been pleased to find. He wasn't too good at rowing. Kathy waved as long as she could see her mother and father, but the tall grass soon hid them and the car.

"We can still see the hill though," said Kathy, turning her head.

"Sure," said David. "Look at the big crab, Kath. Over there."

A great red-and-blue crab was swimming along just under the surface of the muddy water. It stuck up one wicked-looking claw in a sort of salute and then disappeared. All around them the water was dimpled and dotted where a tremendous swarm of tiny fishes surfaced briefly and then swished away.

"Minnows," stated David. "Or do they have minnows in salt water?"

He pushed with the pole and the boat floated gently in and out between the clumps of reeds. The water gurgled against the wooden sides, a fish leaped up with a tiny splash, but otherwise it was totally silent. David thrust his pole into a tuft of weeds, and something flew up with a muffled squawk.

"What was that?" asked Kathy, startled.

And as if in answer, there arose from a short distance away a loud and indignant "Clack, clack,

51

clack, clack!" Almost at once, every clump of reeds seemed to echo the noise. "Clack, clack, clack, clack!" rose deafeningly from all sides.

David and Kathy stared at each other. At length the racket died away, only now and then a faint clack-clack sounding out like an afterthought.

"What in the world was that?" asked Kathy. "A dragon? Or a robot man who needed oiling?"

"I don't know," David answered. "But I'd say there were a good many of them. I know one thing —I'm not going to go poking in any more reeds."

"If you think men from Mars are invading the marsh, I'll be glad to put lanterns on Crossbone Hill," Kathy said. "You know, one if by land, two if by sea."

But David wasn't listening. He was debating between looking for the Northwest Passage and searching for the Seven Cities of Cibola. In the end he adjusted his armor and followed his *adelantado,* because of the gold. He needed money for his mother's birthday present. And just beyond this marsh was a city with streets of gold. He shoved harder with the pole.

Kathy wasn't any help though. She kept taking

off her hat and asking him if he didn't think her hair was getting curlier. He ignored her as long as he could. Finally, he had to give up being a member of De Soto's expedition.

"Are you crazy?" he asked her. "Why would your hair be any curlier than it was yesterday?"

"Well, Mary Jane Campbell went to the beach and when she got back, her hair was curly," said Kathy. "With curly hair I might be a movie star."

"I'll bet Mary Jane's mother gave her a permanent wave," David said scornfully. He raised his pole and pointed. "Look, let's go over there where the trees are and eat lunch in the shade."

Kathy agreed and David maneuvered the boat up to the trees.

"It's awfully swampy and mosquitery-looking," commented Kathy, staring into the shadowy depths where vines and mosses looped from tree to tree, making dim and mysterious tunnels where the water wound in and out.

A big white egret swooped down in front of them and sailed into the dimness. It did look strange and a little frightening.

"Well, we can eat here anyway," said David. He

would like to explore in among the live oaks. That would be a real adventure. He'd ask his father to go with him next time. Or maybe if he could get away from Kathy, he'd go alone.

There was some trouble getting out the lunch and dividing it. There didn't seem to be any place to put cups and sandwiches in the boat, and somehow all the paper napkins fell in the water. But, as David said, "Who needs napkins?"

They ate the sandwiches, apples, and cookies and drank the lemonade. They sat for some time afterward, feeling full and lazy, watching the sun glitter on the water and hearing all the queer little splashes and clicks and mutters in the mud and reeds.

Kathy turned and stared into the gloom. "Let's go in just a little way, Dave," she suggested.

He picked up the pole. Cautiously he pushed the boat along one of the channels of water. Long fringes of moss slithered over their heads.

"Isn't this exciting?" whispered Kathy. "Oh, I'm scared. And David, look! The water's turned a horrible ugh-green."

"That's just a reflection of those vines, silly," David told her. "Hey, there's a bird's nest. Shall we take it to Mother?"

Kathy stretched up her arm and felt around inside the nest. "It's empty," she said.

"Well, get it then," David told her. "It may be a kind she's never seen before."

Kathy took hold of the nest and tugged gently. "Oh, pooh, it busted," she said in disgust. She looked at the half a nest in her hand. "There's a piece of paper woven into it."

She drew out a crumpled yellow scrap, showering twigs and mud all over her knees and legs, and spread it out. She sat a minute staring at it, and finally she gave a queer sort of moaning gulp.

"What's the matter?" asked David. "Did you swallow a mosquito?"

Kathy's eyes were dark and big in the shadows. "It's a map," she whispered at last. "A pirate map of the marsh and the place where treasure is buried!"

Chapter 4

"**D**ON'T BE A CREEP," David growled. "I'm too old to play games like pirate treasure."

"But it's not a g-game," stammered Kathy. "L-look right here!"

She leaned forward and handed the yellowed paper to David. He took it carefully and gently spread it out on his palm. It might not be a treasure map, but there was no sense in busting it up before he found out for sure himself.

The ink was faint, but it hadn't run or streaked. "SWAMP" it said in big scraggly letters. Various lines and circles sprawled over the paper. There was a round circle labeled "ssbone Hill," with the first letters torn away. And right next to the "A" in swamp was a tiny cross and some words.

"You see," Kathy breathed. "There by the cross it says 'pirate rubies.' Rubies are my birthstone. Oh, I just can't wait to find them."

"It doesn't say 'pirate rubies,'" David contradicted. "It says 'pira' and a squiggle and 'rub' and a squiggle." He was arguing, but he couldn't help feeling excited. It looked like one of Kathy's crazy ideas was going to work out. Pirate treasure! Oh, boy! Jewels and doubloons and pieces of eight, spilling out of an old iron chest. He could throw away his old bike, new tires and all, and buy an English racer. Two of them, probably.

"What else could 'pira,' 'rub,' and squiggles mean but 'pirate rubies'?" cried Kathy. "And Dave, it's right here in the marsh! That must be Crossbone Hill. Oh, don't you see, it *has* to be pirates."

David studied the paper for a few minutes more. "I believe you're right," he said at last. "Anyway, there's something hidden here in the marsh. Or why would anybody bother to make a map?"

"Oh, David, let's go look *now!*" squealed Kathy.

"Keep calm, bird brain," he told her. "Let's don't

58

rush into this." He turned the map this way and that. "It's hard to know what's north and what's south on this faded old map. But I think probably the treasure is back in the trees, inside the swamp, and not in the marsh."

Kathy's face fell. "But we can't go in any further," she moaned. "We promised Daddy we wouldn't go where we couldn't see Crossbone Hill."

David pondered. "We said we wouldn't go in the boat," he told her. "But there's a lot of solid ground in there. We could tie the boat here at the edge and walk in if your blisters can stand it."

"I'll speak to them sternly," said Kathy with a smile. "And for rubies, they'll walk."

"We couldn't get lost, because the road to Digby runs right through the middle of the swamp," David went on. "And with my compass and general all-around cleverness, we shouldn't have any trouble."

"All right, let's go now," urged Kathy.

Once more David looked the map over carefully. He picked up the pole and shoved the boat out into the more open water and studied his surroundings thoughtfully. Over his shoulder he could see the queer top of Crossbone Hill standing out against the cloudless blue sky. And straight ahead of him was the shadowy tangle of the swamp. Slowly he worked the boat this way and that, till he had it and the hill aligned in what he assumed was the proper direction.

"Right in there, Kath," he said, pointing. "It ought to be right straight back there, according to the map."

"By that big dead tree?" asked Kathy.

"That's right," agreed David.

"Well, hurry," she cried, but David shook his head.

"It's almost two thirty," he told her. "We'll have to go back. But listen, Kath, we'll mark this place some way so we can find it quickly when we come back. And tomorrow we'll start early, and by lunch time I expect we'll be rich."

"Oh, David, let's go look right now," wailed Kathy. "I'm sure it won't take a minute."

But David was firm. "If we were late getting back, Mother and Daddy might not let us come tomorrow. Besides," he added practically, "if the tide left us stranded, we'd have to wade back. And I expect this mud's full of all kinds of creepy, crawly

60

things, to say nothing of crabs like that big one we saw this morning."

"Let's go back now, quick," said Kathy, staring uneasily down into the water.

David grinned at her. "We got to mark this place first," he said.

Kathy drew a bright-red ribbon out of her shirt pocket. It had started out as a hair ribbon, but like all of Kathy's ribbons it had slipped out of her hair. She had chewed on one end for a while until Dave had observed that the dye was staining her chin pink. So it was somewhat bedraggled, but still dazzlingly red and useful.

Dave tied it to a bush and then pushed the boat away from the trees and off through the marsh toward the causeway. "That's very good," he stated, looking back. "You can see it, but only if you're looking for it—if you know what I mean."

As the boat slid through the clumps of grass Kathy made plans for the next day. "Don't let's say anything to Mother and Daddy about this," she suggested. "Let's just surprise them when we walk in with our pockets stuffed full of gold and rubies. And they'll ask where we got such wealth, and we'll say that some little bird told us. And they won't believe it, but it'll be true."

David laughed and then sobered. "We won't tell them, in case it turns out that there isn't any treasure. There's no use letting them get their hopes up and then be disappointed," he said.

"Oh, David, there is a treasure, there is, there is!" insisted Kathy.

"Well, keep still about it. Voices carry across water, and there's Daddy," he told her.

Mr. Vance was waiting at the edge of the marsh. The children weren't late, but nevertheless the water had ebbed away from the spot where the boat was usually tied. David had to jump out and push it the last couple of feet. Sure enough, the mud was full of creepy, crawly things or at least it felt that way. He was relieved when he finally emerged with all his toes intact.

"Well, Captain Cook and Miss Cook," Mr. Vance bellowed in a deep voice, "just tell us in a few brief words a little something about the strange and wonderful lands you have visited during your extended voyage up the Orinoco and down the Nile. Did you see unipeds? Men with tails? Krakens? Mermen?

Vegetable sheep? Come, come, sirs, don't just stand there. Unfold your tale of perils and horrors."

"Oh, Daddy!" giggled Kathy. "What are unipeds anyway? We only saw crabs and herons and things like that."

David tried to get Kathy to look at him so he could warn her again not to say anything about the map. But before he could do it, Mr. Vance was hustling them toward the car where their mother was waiting.

"Come along," he cried. "I want to get up to Digby and get my tire fixed. And since Digby is not the swiftest-moving metropolitan center I ever ran into, I imagine it'll take some time."

He was right. The garage at Digby was a very relaxing place. Nobody seemed in a hurry, and everybody was eager to talk. There was quite a long discussion of what could possibly have caused the flat tire before it occurred to anybody to look and see. When the puncture was finally located, there was another discussion of what should be done about it.

Standing in the soft dust at the edge of the road, David and Kathy each drank a gigantic orange soda. Mrs. Vance watched some infinitesimal birds in a live-oak tree. "Parula warblers," she murmured. "Aren't they beautiful?"

"Gosh," David muttered to his sister. "I didn't think they had warblers at the seashore. But I guess you don't ever get away from them." He suffered another twinge of conscience over the lost bird-book.

Mr. Vance, who was sitting in the car reading a book, looked up just then and called out, "Why don't you two go into that little shop over there? They've got some nice shells."

The shop was located halfway between the garage and the grocery store, which together with six houses, a small church, and a motel made up the town of Digby. Gold letters on the shop's window said: Postcards—Souvenirs—Curiosities.

Inside, David drew a deep breath of satisfaction. "Neat," he said.

The big windows and whitewashed walls made the place look clean and airy and light. There were mounted fish on the walls and a king crab as big as a washtub and many varieties of starfish. Ropes and nets and hammocks were coiled and folded on the floor. Glass cases full of shells of all sorts and sizes, sea urchins ranging from monsters down to one no bigger than a dime, crabs, coral, and seaweed were ranged around the room.

"Oh, look at these shells!" cried Kathy. "They look like feathers. And see the pink ones!"

"I like the crab with the goosebumps or barnacles or whatever they are all over him," commented David. "And look at that crazy red-and-white one."

"They've got such awful claws," Kathy said, with a shiver. "Oh, what a dear little sea horse!"

They spent some minutes looking at the curious creatures in the cases and were absorbed in a display of conch shells when the sound of footsteps made them look up.

An elderly gentleman stood in the doorway. He was a big man, tall and broad, with snow-white hair and skin burned so dark it made his hair look quite dazzling. His clothes were clean but somewhat ragged, and on his feet he wore rope sandals.

In one hand he held a long, shining gray object and now he stepped forward and swung this thing up onto one of the glass cases. "Good afternoon," he said politely to the children.

Kathy gasped and even David couldn't resist asking, "Please, sir, is that thing a fish?"

The man smiled. "No, it isn't really a fish. It's an elasmobranch," he told them. He held it up so they could see it—a strange, smooth beast about two feet long, with curved fins and a wide hammer-shaped head.

"It looks like a shark," ventured David.

The man beamed at him. "You are exactly right," he nodded.

"But a shark's a fish," persisted David.

The man shook his head. "No, a fish has a bony skeleton. A shark's structure is composed of cartilage, rather like what your ear is made of. He's a very primitive fellow and a very interesting one. Notice the eyes at each end of the hammerlike head. Startling, wouldn't you say?"

"What are you going to do with it?" asked David.

"I sometimes catch one of these young sharks when I'm fishing," explained the man. "If it's an unusual one, like this hammerhead, I bring it to the man who runs this shop, and he stuffs it and sells it to some tourist at a shocking price."

"Oh," remarked David. "What are those cuts in its side?"

The gentleman turned the shark over and looked

66

where David was pointing. "Those aren't cuts; those are its gill openings," he stated. "A fish is quite differently constructed, with gill covers, but elasmobranchs simply have these gill slits, five usually, sometimes six or seven of them."

"Jeepers," said David, "I guess you know a lot about sea things."

"I am not uninformed along those lines," answered the man with a slight bow.

Kathy almost giggled. "Well, then tell us the names of some of these things," she cried, pointing into the cases. "What's that shell down there?"

"That?" questioned the man. "Why, that's a *Fasciolaria distans.*"

Kathy stared. "Doesn't it have any other name?" she wanted to know.

The gentleman looked thoughtfully into space for a moment. "I suppose it has, but I never happened to learn it," he admitted. He rubbed his chin and stared down at Kathy as though he'd only just seen her. "Where did you come from, child?" he asked suddenly. "You don't live around here, I'm sure. And the tourist season hasn't yet started."

"I guess we got it started a little early, sir," explained David. "We're staying in Dr. Dwight's old house, down near the inlet."

"Dr. Dwight's!" the gentleman cried out. For a minute he stared at the children and then his face flushed dark-red. "Well, let me tell you both one thing—let me warn you . . ." He paused and shook his finger at them. "Don't go into the swamp! Whatever you do, don't go into the swamp!"

He picked up the shark and stalked across the shop and out a little door at the back.

Chapter 5

DAVID AND KATHY stared at each other. "He knows," Kathy whispered. "Oh, David, he knows about the treasure, and he's trying to keep us from finding it!"

"I . . . I guess so," David answered. "He sure sounded mad. I wonder how *he* found out about the treasure."

"Well, anyway, it's us that's got the map," began Kathy, when David interrupted. "Pipe down," he warned. "Somebody's coming!"

A stout, kindly looking woman came in the door through which the gentleman and the shark had gone out. "Hello, chicks," she said with a smile. "Can I help you?"

"No'm, thanks, not today," David muttered, backing toward the entrance. "We were just looking, thanks." He grabbed Kathy and dragged her along with him as he stumbled out of the shop.

"Well, for pity's sake," exclaimed Kathy, rubbing her arm where David had seized her. "I suppose you think that didn't look suspicious."

"Maybe so," said David. "But you know what I think? I think that old man sent her in to find out what we know. And you know how you are, Kath. You can't keep a secret."

"I can too," Kathy protested. "It's just that nobody ever tells me any secrets."

"Come along," Mother called. "We're ready to leave, Dave. Hop in the car, Kath."

Once again David seized Kathy's arm. "Well, you know a secret now—a good one. And don't you breathe a word to anybody, Kath, or I'll . . . I'll drown your doll collection."

Kathy's eyes opened wide. "This is *my* secret, more than it is yours, David Vance," she cried. "After all, who said there was treasure here? *Me!* Who found the map? *Me!*"

"There you go," groaned David, slapping his fore-

71

head. "Blabbing it to the whole wide world. Now be quiet, will you."

Kathy flounced to the car, and all the way home she sat in sulky silence. But by suppertime she was as lively and talkative as ever and seemed to have forgotten all about pirates and treasure and everything connected with them.

"I'm sorry the ice cream's a little sloppy," said Mrs. Vance, handing around the bowls. "An old-fashioned icebox doesn't keep it hard very long."

"Chocolate ripple," murmured Kathy. "My favorite."

"I like it kind of mushy," David told his mother. "Did you get it at Digby?"

His mother nodded. "Yes, in the grocery store there. Oh, I forgot to tell you. There was a man in the store, and he had a little hammerhead shark he'd caught. Such a queer-looking beast. I wanted you to see it, but he went off before I could call you."

David shot Kathy an anxious glare. She took a spoonful of ice cream and looked blissful and innocent. "Maybe we'll catch one some time," he said hastily. He cast about for some other topic of conversation, but the one he found was the wrong one.

72

"How did you get along with your work today?" he asked his father politely.

Mr. Vance looked surprised. "I'm happy to say it went very well indeed," he replied. "And how did your marsh exploration go? Did you find anything

exciting, like a shrunken pelican's head or a dinosaur soup bone?"

"We found a bird's nest," cried Kathy, and David groaned inwardly. But he needn't have worried. Mr. Vance suddenly pushed back his bowl and stood up.

"Let's hurry and help Mother with the dishes and get to bed. I got up early this morning and had a swim before breakfast, and I'm tired from head to toe."

"Saved by the bell," David thought, and for once in his life he was delighted to go to bed. Having a secret with a girl was awful, worse than playing baseball with girls. You never knew what they were going to do.

He'd only been asleep an hour or so when somebody shook him awake. "David," whispered Kathy. "David! Wake up! Somebody's stealing our treasure."

David stared at the dim form bending over him. "You walking in your sleep or something? What's the matter with you, Kath?" he asked, yawning.

"Oh, David, come see," begged Kathy, pulling at him. "And be quiet."

Reluctantly David swung his feet over the edge of the bed and stood up. He bumped into the dresser and said, "Ow!"

"Shh!" cautioned Kathy, and she took him by the hand and led him silently through the living

74

room and out onto the screened porch. "Look!" she whispered.

There was a light shining out of the darkness halfway between heaven and earth, like a lost star.

It blinked and then came on, blinked out again, and then shone steadily.

"See," said Kathy, "it's on the hill—Crossbone Hill."

David nodded in the dark. It must be on the hill.

"And those are the other pirates over there," Kathy told him, giving him a poke in the ribs.

Sure enough, there was an answering light from the swamp, a flicker as faint as a lightning bug's flash.

"They're after the treasure," Kathy cried softly. "And they're signaling to each other. Oh, David, we've got to do something!"

"Well, I don't think there's anything we can do, here in the middle of the night," David answered. "Besides, they can't know where the treasure is. We've got the map. But Kath, we'll have to go first thing in the morning and see if we can locate the rubies. Because they may not have the map, but they're awful close to the spot."

"Oh, dear, oh, dear," sighed Kathy. "I just hate pirates."

"Those aren't pirates, silly," David told her. "There aren't any pirates nowadays. How did you happen to see these lights?"

There was a minute's embarrassed silence. "I got up to look at the tidal wave," said Kathy.

"What?" exclaimed David.

"Well, you know, Daddy was telling us about tidal waves that time," Kathy went on. "And I woke up and I was thinking about it, and I was just *sure* all the water was being sucked out to sea to come back as a tidal wave thirty feet high. So I got up to see. And that's when I saw the lights."

"Tidal waves and pirates," snickered David. "Last month it was vampires and werewolves. Your head goes round so much it's a wonder it hasn't screwed off your back. Oh, well, we'd better get back to bed if we want to leave for the swamp early tomorrow morning."

Kathy padded off, and David groped his way back to his own bed. But once there he found he was chilly and uncomfortable and excited, too. He lay awake listening to the regular roar and whoosh of the waves and wondering who could be after the treasure. Gangsters maybe?

He stirred uneasily. He liked to think he was as brave as most boys, but he didn't believe he could do much against gangsters with submachine guns and sawed-off shotguns and all.

And Kathy—maybe he ought not to let Kathy go to the swamp at all if it was going to be dangerous.

77

But he had a definite feeling it wouldn't be easy to leave her behind.

He'd have to smuggle a shovel into the boat somehow. He'd seen a shovel in a little tool shed under the house. He ought to get it right now, while everybody was asleep, and hide it away from the house, for it would never do if his parents saw him leave with the shovel. You don't go exploring in swamps with a shovel, and they'd be suspicious at once.

But he was becoming warm and drowsy now. He hated to get up, and he decided he needn't bother. He and Kathy would be clever enough to work out something in the morning. He pulled the blanket up to his chin and was asleep.

David had been awake a good while nevertheless. And next morning the sun was high and his father already gone when he heard his mother calling.

"Get up, Dave, and come eat breakfast. I've got big plans for today."

David's heart sank. Big plans! Whatever they were, David knew they weren't the same as his.

Chapter 6

WITH HIS T-SHIRT over his head and his arms waving wildly, David appeared at the kitchen door. "What plans?" he asked in a muffled voice.

"Well," said Mrs. Vance, "as soon as you've finished dressing—and I must say, considering how few clothes you wear, it does look as though you could put them on before you come to the table—as soon as you've finished dressing and eating breakfast and have made your beds, we're going crabbing."

"Crabbing?" asked Dave, settling his T-shirt and sliding into his place at the table. "What for?"

"Crabs," answered Mrs. Vance.

"Very funny," said David grimly. "Who's going to cook them? You?"

Mrs. Vance recoiled. "Gracious no!" she exclaimed. "But the man who runs the filling station told me one of the boardinghouses on the beach above Digby is open, and the woman who runs it will be glad to cook the crabs for us and serve us a meal of them. I thought it would be a nice change from Vienna sausages and hard-boiled eggs."

David ate his cereal in silence. Privately, he thought it would be wonderful. He'd never dreamed he could get tired of Vienna sausages so soon.

"But I'd live on them a long time before I'd give up those pirate rubies," he thought. "I wish Mother had waited one more day to have this brain storm. If we could just get back in the swamp, I know I could find the place. I *know* I could."

"Where's Kath?" he asked aloud.

"She's outside getting the crab nets untangled," his mother told him. "And by the way, your father left you a message. He wants you to quit riding elephants through the house at night and shouting at the poor beasts when they make a wrong turn. And I want to know what you were really doing up in the middle of the night."

Dave grinned. He hoped his father hadn't over-

80

heard anything important. "Kathy thought there was going to be a tidal wave," he explained. "She was sure she heard the ocean being sucked out to sea."

"And that's true," he thought. "That is what got her up."

"Well, I'm glad she woke you and Daddy, and not me," said Mother. "One thing about tramping up and down the beach bird-watching, it really makes you sleep at night. If you've finished breakfast, run make your bed and we'll go."

As he pulled up his sheets and made an attempt to smooth out the wrinkles, David considered every possibility for getting out of this expedition. He would say he was sick, and he'd rub soap over his tongue so that when his mother looked in his mouth it would be coated. But she would be sure to give him some horrible-tasting medicine and stay right here with him. That wouldn't do. And she wouldn't like it; she'd surely get suspicious if he said he wanted to stay home and read a book or something.

There was no way out. He would have to go, but he would catch a lot of crabs as quickly as he could, and then get away. He and Kathy would pick up the shovel and head for the swamp as soon as they could possibly make it.

He ran out of his room and through the kitchen. Mother and Kath were standing at the foot of the back steps with a bushel basket, some lines with hooks and sinkers, a damp bundle of newspaper, and two butterfly nets. At least they looked like butterfly nets to David.

"Well, for Pete's sake! Flying crabs?" he asked.

Mrs. Vance laughed. "No," she replied. "The crabs are regulation variety. But this is the way it's done. Come along and I'll show you."

Some distance down the road a rickety wooden pier ran out into the muddy water of the marsh. At the end there was a small roofed platform with rough benches around the sides. Here the procession of Vances stopped. Mrs. Vance opened the damp newspaper and took out a chunk of raw meat.

"Ugh!" said Kathy, holding her stomach.

"Never mind!" said Mrs. Vance, looking severe. She ran the hook into the meat and dropped the line into the water. Handing the other end to David, she said, "Now just wait till you feel something tugging on your line; then pull up slowly till you can see the crab, and I'll get the net under him and haul him up."

"Oh, is that all?" asked David, a little disappointed.

"Well, there are apt to be complications," Mrs. Vance assured him as she baited the other lines. "Just don't fall in the water, that's all I ask. I know it's only waist-deep, but I'm convinced whole families of Loch Ness monsters live in the mud at the bottom, and I'm petrified at the idea of falling in."

David looked around at the mud and stiff grass and the rotting posts where piers had once been. It looked so desolate he doubted that any self-respecting monster would live here. And as the morning passed and nothing happened, he began to doubt that any crabs lived here either.

The sky was blue and cloudless, the sun grew higher and hotter, the wind rustled the reeds and made a million ripples in the brown water. David felt something pulling at one of his lines and he raised it slowly, but there was nothing there.

He sighed. This was even duller than fishing. He'd been fishing a time or two with his grandfather and found it pretty boring. But at least then you could change from one bait to another and give yourself something to do, or see how far you could cast artificial minnows. But here there was nothing to do but dangle your heels.

And all the time he was hot inside with impatience because somebody else was out digging up the treasure that rightfully belonged to the Vances. How much longer would his mother keep them here? he wondered.

"There goes one of those terms, Mother," murmured Kathy.

"Terns, dopey—'n' not 'm,'" growled David. "What makes you so stupid?"

"Yes, it is a tern, Kathy," said Mother. "A least tern, and you were clever to recognize him. Don't be so superior, David. It wasn't so long ago you used to call 'vanilla,' 'banilla.' Remember?"

David glared at the slender white bird skimming over his head, and said nothing. He was hot and angry and bored with crabbing. When Kathy brushed against him a minute later, he pushed her away and snarled, "Don't keep stepping all over me!"

Kathy turned around, ready for battle, when suddenly her eyes grew big. "I've got one," she whispered. "I've got one!"

"Where? Where?" cried Mrs. Vance, brandishing the net.

"Here," answered Kathy, drawing up one line.

"Not so fast," warned Mrs. Vance. "Here, David, take the net. Get it under him. Don't pull up the line any more, Kathy."

"Oh, quick," moaned Kathy. "He's wiggling his legs! Quick, quick!"

"Don't push!" shouted David, swapping the net from hand to hand.

"Watch out," exclaimed Mrs. Vance.

"Quick, quick!" yelled Kathy.

"Got him! I got him," David chortled as he made a swoop with the net.

"The basket, the basket," gasped Mrs. Vance.

"Oh, oh, oh," squealed Kathy in anguish. "He'll get away."

David brought the net up over the basket and shook it vigorously. "He won't let go the net," he shouted.

Kathy danced around poking at the net.

"Watch out for your fingers!" cried Mrs. Vance.

"Oh, oh, oh," screamed Kathy.

David whanged the net on the edge of the basket, and the crab dropped in.

Kathy bent over and stared. "He's so little," she cried. "I thought he was a giant."

David collapsed on a bench, and Mrs. Vance

laughed and laughed. "We made enough noise for several giants," she said weakly. "But he's only the beginning. As soon as one bites, the others start. So tend to your lines."

Sure enough something now pulled at one of Dave's lines. It was a whopper when it was finally dropped in the basket, where it calmly proceeded to snap off the legs of Kathy's crab.

"Oh, the mean old thing!" cried Kathy. "Mother, do something. Oh, oh, I've got another one!"

And in an hour they had the basket almost full of crabs. There had been a great deal of screaming and squealing. David had had his finger nipped twice, and Kathy had a large bruise on her chin from hitting herself with the net.

David sat on one of the benches, panting. It had been a most exciting morning. And there was still plenty of time to get back into the swamp and look for the treasure.

"Now," said Mrs. Vance, looking at her watch, "in twenty minutes Mrs. Hale's truck will pick up the crabs. I'm going on home, and you two take the basket and walk up to the crossroads and wait for the truck."

David gave Kathy a despairing look. "You'd think Mother knew about the treasure and was just trying to keep us from getting it," he told himself.

"What's the matter?" asked Mrs. Vance. "Am I interfering with other plans? This won't take long, you know. Then you're free to do what you like. Come back and swim with me if you want to. Or go exploring or shell-gathering."

"Well, would it be all right if we didn't come straight back, but did some exploring on the way home?" Dave asked.

Mrs. Vance frowned a little. Finally she said, "Well, don't be gone too long." Then suddenly she smiled. "Oh, David, it is hard for me to remember you're big enough to go off on your own in a strange place. Be back by one, and remember Kathy's younger and littler than you. Don't wear her out."

She walked away down the pier, and the children followed with the basket of crabs.

"Well, I like that," Kathy grumbled. "I can't help being younger and littler. I can run faster than anybody in my class, even the boys. I never get tired."

"If you're so energetic, carry your share of the

basket," said David. "The crabs are all sliding over on my side."

When they reached the road Mrs. Vance turned and walked toward the house, stopping every now and then to examine some bird with her field glasses. David and Kathy trudged up the sandy road till they were well out of earshot.

"Anyway, we'll have time to go into the swamp from the Digby road and see if we can get our bearings," David said. "I sure hate to put it off any longer, Kath, digging for the rubies, I mean. But if we go back for the shovel, the day will be over by the time we get it in the boat and back to the hairribbon place."

Kathy nodded. "Whee, it's hot," was all she said.

And it was. The sun blazed down, but the air had grown hazy and humid. The sky was no longer pure robin's-egg blue, but almost white. Mosquitoes buzzed and whined around them now they were in among the trees.

In a few minutes they had reached the crossroads where they were to wait for the truck. The crabs made curious sizzling and bubbling noises in their basket, the mosquitoes sang, and Dave wished he had something cold to drink. They didn't have to wait too long before a pickup truck came bumping down the road from Digby. It stopped and a tall slender Negro boy got out.

"These Mrs. Vance's crabs?" he asked in a soft voice. "The ones for Mrs. Hale?"

"Yes," answered David.

The Negro boy smiled and swung the basket into the back of the truck. "Mrs. Hale says they'll be waiting for you tomorrow," he told them. "Dinner's at one o'clock."

The truck slewed around and bounced back the way it had come. As soon as the trail of dust had settled, Dave started down the road. He peered into the undergrowth and Kathy did too. She gave a little shiver.

"I wish it didn't look so *snaky*," she said.

"Oh, don't be such a fuss-budget, Kath," said David, glancing uneasily under a bush. "Just don't step over any logs without looking first. Here's a kind of path. Let's go a little way along it."

They stepped in among the undergrowth, and the gloom closed in. Gnats and mosquitoes swarmed about them, and long trailers of Spanish moss dangled from every tree limb. Bushes with dark heavy leaves pushed against them, and the squelchy mud underfoot was streaked with green algae.

David stopped. Somehow the swamp seemed dimmer and stranger than he had expected. He began to speak, and his voice sounded loud and unfamiliar.

"Now the way I figure it, that old man knew somehow that we were after the treasure, so he and his gang tried to get it last night," he explained to Kathy. "Only they didn't have the map. But they must have some idea where it is, and we'll have to find it quickly if we expect to get to it before they do. And we'll have to be careful. The gangsters probably have all kinds of guns."

"*Gangsters?*" repeated Kathy. "That old man didn't look like a gangster to me."

"Well, he didn't look like a pirate either, did he?" David wanted to know. "Besides, I keep telling you, Kathy, there aren't any pirates nowadays."

There was a rustling noise in the bushes. Both children turned to look. Suddenly among the swaying moss and shadowy leaves a gaunt dark face was staring straight at them, with cruel black eyes over a beak of a nose. From one ear dangled a single, round gold hoop.

A long brown hand and a gnarled finger pointed at them, and a harsh voice screamed in the stillness, "Go 'way, bad childrens, go 'way!"

Chapter 7

KATHY WAS RIGHT, David thought. She could really run. By the time he burst out of the bushes into the road, she was almost back to the crossroads. Her feet flew along in the soft dust, and David was so interested in watching her he forgot what a scare he'd had in the swamp, and slowed to a walk. So when Kathy finally collapsed in the road, it took him several minutes to catch up with her.

"Gosh, Kath," he said admiringly. "I believe you could do better than the four-minute mile."

Color began to creep back into her white cheeks. "D-did you s-see him?" she stammered. "If he wasn't a p-p-pirate, what was he?"

"He sure looked like one," Dave confessed. He thought a minute. "I wish we hadn't run. I wish we'd stayed and found out something about him."

"Not me," said Kathy firmly. "I don't want to walk the plank. Besides, I couldn't help running. My legs just worked without me even knowing it."

"I guess that's the way it was with me, too," David said sheepishly. "Who do you reckon he was? He was fierce-looking, all right." He glanced over his shoulder, but no one else was in sight. At least the pirate hadn't run after them. In fact, now that it was all over it was a little hard to believe in him, because he *had* looked just like a pirate, like an illustration for *Treasure Island,* gold earring and all.

"Oh, David," wailed Kathy. "We're never going to get the treasure. With that old man with the shark after it, and this pirate guarding it, we'll never be able to dig it up. And I wanted a ruby so much."

"Listen, Kath, we've got to run for home," said David. "No wonder it was so dark in the swamp. Look at those clouds. It's going to pour in a few minutes."

Kathy looked up. The white haze that had blanketed the sky earlier had deepened and darkened to a thick gray cover overhead. The sultry air was still, with the waiting stillness that means a storm. And thunder rumbled faintly to the south.

Kathy got up out of the dust, and they set off down the road. As they walked David pondered. Perhaps he ought to tell his father about the treasure. Somehow though, talk about pirates and treasure and gangsters that sounded fine when he was discussing things with Kathy only sounded corny when he thought about telling his father.

But something mysterious was going on in the swamp. Everything that had happened to them since they had come here had been mysterious—the map, the old man's warning, the lights, the pirate, even the disappearance of the blue bird-book.

And what were they going to do now—give up?

"No," David told himself. "I'm going to get into that swamp and see what the secret is, or bust. But next time I go, I'm going to leave Kathy at home; I know that. I can get along better by myself."

Lightning streaked down the sky, and now the wind began to blow in big gusts that laid the reeds and grasses almost flat and sent the dust swirling.

"Rubies are my birthstone," said Kathy with a sniff. "I hate to quit without finding even one. But I'm scared of pirates; I really am."

"I'd rather never have a ruby than have my throat cut," agreed David. And he glanced at her out of the corner of his eye. That ought to fix her. She'd really be too scared to go into the swamp now. A heavy drop of rain hit him squarely in the center of his crew cut.

"We'd better run," said Kath, and they ran. The rain pelted down in big slow drops, and by the time they reached the house David's T-shirt was thoroughly wet and Kathy's hair was streaming.

"Howdy, strangers," Mrs. Vance greeted them. "I'm proud to see you. I didn't know what I was going to do if it started to storm and you two hadn't come back."

"Mother," cried Kathy. "You really don't think we've got sense enough to come in out of the rain."

Mrs. Vance laughed. "Kathy, I've been caught out bird-watching in the rain often enough myself to know how easy it is to ignore the weather till it's too late. Goodness, what a streak of lightning."

Seconds later thunder shook the little house, and the rain became a torrent. The wind banged the doors and set the window shades rattling.

"Quick!" called Mrs. Vance. "Close the windows. The rain's just pouring in."

The windows, which had been hard to open, were almost impossible to shut. In fact, David's window refused to go the last half foot, and he had to stuff towels and dirty clothes and newspaper in the space to keep out the water.

"Kathy, you're wet," Mrs. Vance exclaimed. "Go dry your hair and change your shirt while I light a fire. Then we'll have lunch."

Lunch was bacon and eggs, toast and cocoa. David wondered why these things, which always tasted so flat and uninteresting at breakfast, made such a delicious lunch as they sat in front of the fireplace, with the wind howling outside and the surf pounding and roaring on the beach. It grew so dark they had to light a lamp.

"Now this is certainly cozy," said Mrs. Vance, throwing the paper plates into the fire. "Heavens, listen to that wind. Have you each got something good to read? Or shall we play a game?"

"Monopoly!" cried Kathy, and David agreed.

It took some time to find the board and the pieces, and assemble table and chairs. They had just got things set up and Kathy was dealing out the money, when her mother looked up, startled. "Did you hear that noise?" she asked.

"What noise?" Kathy said in a whisper.

The fire blazed up and shadows grew long and wobbly in the big room. The house creaked in the wind.

"The pirate," thought David. "He's come through the storm after us." And thoughts of long daggers and Jolly Rogers whirled in his head.

Someone was certainly fumbling at the back door. And then the door was hurriedly pushed open and slammed to, and Mr. Vance's voice called out, "Hello, the house! Any drowned bodies here? Ah, cocoa! Just what I wanted. What no marshmallows? An unforgivable oversight! What on earth shall I do with my jacket? I think I've got fishes in the pockets, it's so wet."

They crowded around him. "What are you doing home so early, Phil?"

"Daddy, I thought you were a pirate!" cried Kathy.

"We've got a fire in the living room," David said. "I'll hang your jacket near it."

Mr. Vance poured himself a cup of cocoa. "I came home early because of the storm. There's always a chance a tree might blow down across the road or something like that, and I didn't want you three to be alone all night. And Kathy, I hate to be found out, but I really am a pirate, you know. You may think I go to the library to do research during the day, but actually I hurry away to a hidden bay and change my clothes. Then in my four-masted schooner I cruise up and down the coastal waters, preying on rich merchants and hearty beachcombers. I'm sorry you found me out, because now I'll have to do away with you, my own daughter. Just let me slip out of these wet clothes and sharpen my dirk."

"Oh, Daddy," giggled Kathy, "we were going to play Monopoly. Will you play too?"

"Sure," he answered. "But just remember what a cutthroat I am. I intend to end up a millionaire."

All during the game the storm increased. Mother went bankrupt almost immediately. She always did, and sometimes David thought she did it on purpose. But he and Kathy and Mr. Vance played on while the wind screamed around the house and the surf sounded as though it were coming up on the front porch.

"Dave," said Mrs. Vance. "Go do something about the screen door on the porch, will you? Every time it bangs like that I jump."

"Yes'm," said David. He got up and opened the door from the living room onto the screened porch. He had to push and shove against the wind to get the door open. And then he had a struggle to pull the screen door to and latch it.

He stood for a moment squinting out into the weather. The blowing sand and the rain and spray

made such a mist he could see only a few feet. The bushes bent to the ground, and every now and then something dark and indescribable went hurtling by on the wind.

"Anyway," David consoled himself, "as long as this weather keeps up, *nobody* will be able to look for anything in the swamp. I wonder if this is a hurricane."

He went back into the house in time to hear Kathy complain, "I don't see why I have to pay income tax. I haven't had any income in I don't know how long."

"I just paid you one hundred and twelve dollars rent," said Mr. Vance. "What do you call income? Your turn, Dave."

David won. He was thinking so hard about the pirate and the treasure, he hardly knew what he was doing, so he kept on buying houses long after he would normally have stopped. The result was that Kathy, who was so cautious about buying that she almost never owned any property, shortly went bankrupt.

"David, you are a master hand at finance," said Mr. Vance, beginning to stack the money into piles. "I don't see why I couldn't have had some of your talent, instead of being so handsome and curly-headed."

David, fitting the houses and hotels into their little box, looked up at his father. "Daddy, do you think pirates might really have left any loot in this section?"

Mr. Vance smiled. "It's possible," he answered. "But I should think finding it would be highly unlikely, even for a financier with a nose for wealth like yours."

David put the top on the box and twisted a rubber band around it. "Well, Daddy," he went on slowly, "suppose there were two kids, like me and Kath, and they found a map and it showed where pirate treasure was buried. And then when they went there, there was a real pirate guarding the treasure; I mean a real pirate with earrings and everything. What would you think?"

"I'd think the children were victims of a practical joke, or hallucinations," replied Mr. Vance. "A map I might believe, but a pirate with earrings, no, not today." And he shook his head.

David thought he might as well show his father the map. For a minute he couldn't think where he'd left it. And then he remembered it was in the pocket of the shorts he'd taken off yesterday.

He got up and went into his room, where the wind and rain still streamed through the open window. Now where had he left his shorts? They ought to be right here in this convenient spot on the floor. But they weren't. Had Mother picked them up and put them in the wash? He hoped not. Frowning, David scanned the room.

Of course! The shorts were stuffed in the open window, damming up the water that flowed in. Well, that wasn't going to help the map. He sprang to snatch them from among the newspapers and damp towels.

The shorts were pretty wet. With a sinking heart, David felt in first one dripping pocket and then another. Finally he drew out a flake or two of damp paper, and then some scraps. And that was all.

Crumpled in the wet pocket, the old map had disintegrated.

Chapter 8

"THE WIND'S SLACKING UP," said Mr. Vance "I'm glad," said Kathy. "I thought we were going to have a hurricane."

"A hurricane! That little breeze?" asked Mr. Vance. "Haven't you ever heard the old rhyme? 'June—too soon'? And if June is too soon for hurricanes, May is clear out of the running. Besides, if there's going to be a hurricane near here, it's known for days ahead and everybody is carried off on the back of a Coast Guardsman."

"Well, I have to admit that wind made me a little nervous, too," spoke up Mrs. Vance. "If that just was a little breeze, I certainly don't want to be here when a big one's going on. Would any one care for any more potato salad?"

"No, thanks," her husband answered. "What time is it, Kath? We seem to have dined at a very fashionable hour."

Kathy peered at the little clock on the mantel. "Seven twenty-two," she announced slowly.

"Ah, I thought so," exclaimed Daddy. "The witching hour, as the saying goes. I could tell it by the twitching of my ear lobes. Now Kathy, run put the rest of the supper in the icebox, and Dave, you put the spoons in the sink. Judith, you sit here, and I, by the uncertain light of the flickering fire, will a tale unfold that will stand your knotted and combined locks clean up to the ceiling."

"Oh, goody, ghost stories!" cried Kathy, and she and David hurried through their chores.

First, Mr. Vance read two of those truly terrifying tales by M. R. James. And then Mrs. Vance said, "Read something more cheerful, will you, Phil? Kathy's sitting so close to me I've hardly got room to breathe."

David had to admit he was glad when Mr. Vance put down the ghost stories. The back of his neck felt uneasy, as though eyes were fastened on it from the gloomy corner, and goose bumps rose on his arms every time the fire made shadows dart and swing across the room.

Then Mr. Vance read a hilarious story from *John Gayther's Garden* about pirates and deep-sea diving, and Kathy laughed till she got the hiccups.

"Bedtime," Mrs. Vance said firmly when the story

was ended. "For all of us, Phil. We're running short of kerosene."

The rain was still streaming in David's window in spite of the towels and newspaper stuffed in the opening, and his bed was damp, so his mother made him a pallet on the living-room floor. And then Kathy had to have one, because she wasn't going to sleep way off there by herself when everybody else was cozily together in the living room.

David found his pallet rather hard, and the light of the dying fire flaring up every now and then worried him. He kept going over and over in his mind about how stupid he had been to let the map get ruined. Probably he could draw it from memory, but he might have forgotten something vital.

He hated to have to tell Kathy. She was generally the one who made mistakes, but he guessed this time he'd have to eat crow.

Still it wouldn't keep them from looking for the treasure, for the hair ribbon would show them where to go. Or would it be there after this storm?

And who was that pirate? And the old man? Who had flashed the light in the swamp? And what had Daddy said about seeing smoke rising from that deserted cabin? Of course, that was where the pirates were staying! Why hadn't he thought of that before? He almost sprang up then and there to go investigate.

Wouldn't morning ever come? He twisted and turned. At last he got up and got into Kathy's bed, which was a lot more comfortable. He wished he'd thought of it sooner. In a few minutes he was asleep, in spite of the steady drumming of the rain and the gusts of wind that still shook the house occasionally.

Next morning he woke early to a world of rainbow mists. The rain and wind had taken themselves off, leaving land and sea wrapped in a gauzy fog. The sun glinted through here and there and gave every indication that the day would be bright and beautiful.

David jumped out of bed. He was working out a plan, and this was the ideal time to carry out the first step of it. He tiptoed into his room and slipped into his clothes. Very quietly he walked through the kitchen, out the back door, and down the steps. There, stooping, he crept under the house to the tool shed. The padlock was open, but Dave held his breath as he gently pushed back the door. The hinge was so rusty it squeaked if you looked at it.

It squeaked a little now, but he only opened the door far enough to pull out the shovel. Halfway out, it slipped from his hand and fell with a dull clump. He waited, expecting his father to come running. But nothing happened. He picked up the shovel and left, not daring to shut the shed door.

Out on the road, the sand underfoot had been beaten firm and hard by the rain except where puddles of muddy water were still standing and had to be waded through. A gull, squawking noisily, flew over his head, and the sound of the surf was loud and heavy even through the fog. The mist was thinning and wherever the sun struck through, a thousand colors sprang up and sparkled in the air.

David selected a spot where grass and bushes grew close to the road and hid the shovel there. "I'll have to mark it," he thought.

He could tie some of the grasses in a significant knot, the way his Boy Scout handbook showed. But it certainly wasn't easy to make a neat knot like the one in the picture. The weeds kept coming up in his hands, and they were too stiff. When he was through, it looked as if a buffalo had wallowed there.

"At least, I'll be able to recognize the spot," he told himself. "I hope nobody else does."

A voice behind him said, "Dave! Whatever are you doing?"

David jumped. "N-nothing, Mother," he stammered. "I couldn't sleep, so I got up to—to look around after the storm."

"Isn't it beautiful?" exclaimed Mrs. Vance. "I got up to bird-watch, but it's almost too misty to see anything. Let's go out on the beach."

They went, with David looking back to be sure his shovel was well-hidden. Out on the beach most of the mist had blown away, but wisps of it lingered everywhere, opalescent as the shells that the heavy surf had scattered thickly over the sand.

"Gosh, the tide's really high," said David.

"Oh, David, look, pelicans!" cried Mrs. Vance. And there, close into the shore went a line of seven big birds.

"Gosh, aren't they ugly!" said David, just as his mother said, "Aren't they beautiful?" the way he knew she would. He watched the birds coming up the beach with their great bills folded down against their necks and their squat legs trailing under the stubby tails. They came, one behind the other, alternately beating their wings and soaring. David was amazed to see that they moved in perfect unison. First the big wings flapped in awkward, laboring

strokes. And then came the long liquid glide, and David could see what his mother meant. The pelicans *were* beautiful then, graceful and fascinating.

For just a minute he wished he didn't have the treasure in the back of his head, worrying him. It was wonderfully cool and fresh out here on the beach with birds hurrying up and down the shore, and the waves pouring over each other and running up on the sand with a hiss, leaving the foam behind. He'd like to stay out here and enjoy it. He wouldn't even mind bird-watching with his mother—over there was a good-sized bird with a chest and stomach so dark that it looked as if it had fallen in the mud.

But David didn't have time for that now. He had to get into the swamp and find out what was going on. It wasn't just the thought of jewels or money, though he supposed being rich would be pleasant, even if his mother probably would make him put it in the bank and not let him spend any of it. No, the thing that bothered him now was plain curiosity. He was crazy to find out what was going on, who the pirate and the old man were, and how close they had come to finding the rubies. He wished he could think up something really clever to do to foil them.

"Let's go home, Dave," said Mother. "I'm anxious for my coffee."

"Sure," David agreed with alacrity. And then as they approached the house, he asked, "How come Daddy hasn't left yet? It must be after eight."

"Why," said Mrs. Vance, "today's Sunday. Daddy will be home all day, and I certainly am glad. Aren't you?"

"Sure, sure," answered David with sinking heart. He'd have a hard time carrying out any plan now. For Daddy would be certain to have some lively plan of his own. He always did.

And today was no exception. "How about that expedition to Crossbone Hill?" he asked at breakfast. "Do you all feel energetic enough for some mountain-climbing this morning?"

"Oh, Daddy, yes," cried Kathy. "It makes me feel all creepy just to think about going there. I just know pirates used to build fires on it. Maybe they even buried a treasure up there."

"Oh, no doubt," Daddy agreed. "And now it's haunted by the ghost of a one-eyed African who had to dig the hole and was murdered so that he would never, never reveal the hiding place. On foggy nights he appears as a blob of blue-and-green phosphorescence hovering about three feet four inches over the top of the hill, and sometimes he appears riding on a long purple hotdog. And mysterious wails and sounds of drums issue from the depths of the marsh."

"Daddy, is that true?" asked Kathy in a whisper.

"Not a word of it," said Mr. Vance cheerfully. "But I thought you might enjoy hearing it. Who's in favor of this dangerous climb?"

"Me," answered David without enthusiasm. He couldn't do anything else. It seemed to him that fate was against him. Every plan he made went awry.

"Then synchronize your watches and be sure your oxygen masks are in order," said Mr. Vance. "And as soon as the dishes are done, we'll leave."

In half an hour the Vances were walking up the road toward Crossbone Hill. Mr. Vance gave a long low whistle when he saw the marsh. "There's a lot of water hereabouts," he observed. "It's almost up to the road. All that rain, I guess. We'll have to wade part of the way, I expect. But nothing daunted the intrepid explorers as they dared the rushing torrent, keeping a sharp eye out for alligators and icebergs." And he led the way out onto the spit of dry land that ended in Crossbone Hill.

"Are there really alligators around here?" asked David.

"In the swamp there are supposed to be a good many," Mr. Vance answered. "But it's like flying saucers. Nobody's ever seen one; he just knows a fellow who's seen one."

"Well, I just hope I never see one," said Kathy. "I know I'd die of fright."

"Cease your worries, lassie." Mr. Vance grinned. "All their teeth have been extracted, and they only eat split-pea soup, provided the peas have been split very, very thin, both lengthwise and crosswise."

"Watch out," warned David, who had run ahead, "we really are going to have to wade."

The water rippled over the sandy path, several inches deep. It was clear, and tiny fishes darted through it.

"What's that?" Kathy asked, pointing to a small dark object scuttling through the water.

"A hermit crab, wearing somebody else's clothes," explained Mrs. Vance. "He hasn't a shell of his own, so he has to find an empty shell no one else wants and use it."

"Ouch, a fish bit me," cried Kathy.

"There goes a gull," said Mrs. Vance dreamily.

"Courage, me hearties," called Mr. Vance. "The end's in sight. Keep tight hold of one another. We'll die together if die we must."

"Was it just the rain that made the tide so much higher than usual?" asked David.

"Well, the rain and the wind certainly helped," Mr. Vance answered. "But I believe this is also what's known as a 'spring tide,' when the gravitational pull of sun and moon work in conjunction to pull the tides up unusually high. Anything else you'd care to know? The names of the three highest peaks in the Andes? A short history of the Etruscan burial urns?"

"Oh, Daddy, don't make fun," said Kathy. "You *do* know a lot."

Daddy smiled and pulled her hair. "Thanks, Princess. I'm only trying to let you know in my gentle fashion that I'm human, and it would be a good deal more sensible to consult an encyclopedia than your fallible old father."

"Where would we get an encyclopedia out here?" asked David.

"Why, haven't you heard of instant encyclopedia? Just add water and it's ready to use," Mr. Vance said. "It so happens I have a jar with me, with the easy twist-off lid."

"Here's the hill," remarked David.

It was certainly not very exciting looking, just a heap of sandy earth covered with coarse grass and scrubby bushes. David scrambled up to the top. He stood a minute, gazing out over the marsh and swamp. A thin trickle of smoke rose up from the trees. He stared at it, hoping nobody else would notice. That was certainly it. Whoever was after the treasure was hiding out in that shack.

When his mother came up, he borrowed one of her pairs of field glasses. He couldn't see much of anything. No one moving about, no sun glinting on rifle barrels, no Jolly Roger flying from the treetops. Only that wisp of smoke rising steadily.

David moved the glasses about. And suddenly he realized he wasn't seeing something else, something he should have been seeing. He searched up and down along the edge of the causeway. But the boat was gone!

Chapter 9

THE MORNING seemed endless to David. His stomach was knotted with impatience to get away—to get into the swamp and see what he could find and plot what he should do next. Whoever had stolen the boat meant to keep him out of the swamp. But they'd have to try harder than that. His mind was made up. He was determined to find out what was going on.

It seemed strange that things he'd looked forward to, like climbing Crossbone Hill and swimming with Daddy, should seem so dull and uninteresting when he was anxious to be doing something else. And then after they finished swimming, and just as he was about to put his dirty shorts back on and get going, his mother knocked on his door and said, "Don't forget to put on clean clothes, Dave. We're going to Mrs. Hale's to eat those crabs."

David gritted his teeth. Wouldn't he ever have a chance to get away? And he had no idea what this queer tide was going to do. He wished he knew more about tides. He wished he knew what to do.

Worry and trouble didn't affect his appetite, however. He was thankful for that. In Mrs. Hale's big, cool dining room, with all its windows opening on the sea, he ate with great enjoyment shrimp cocktail, crab soufflé, fried chicken, salad, green peas, and hot rolls, finishing up with strawberry ice cream and chocolate cupcakes. It was all delicious.

"Dave's had something on his mind all morning," said Mr. Vance. "I believe it was this meal he was looking forward to."

"It sure made a nice change from Vienna sausages," David confessed.

"We'll come often, now that Mrs. Hale is serving meals regularly," Mrs. Vance assured him. "I'm sorry about the Vienna sausages, Dave. But I'm scared to try anything more complicated than scrambled eggs on that kerosene stove. Besides, this is supposed to be a vacation for me, too."

"Aw, Mom, I like Vienna sausages," said David. "I don't mind eating them. They've just gotten a little monotonous, that's all."

Mr. and Mrs. Vance laughed, and in a few minutes they were all back in the car on the way home. David gave a sigh of relief. In another twenty minutes he'd be headed for that "deserted" shack, ready to spy out what was really going on. That was his only chance, now that the boat was missing.

But once again it looked as though he was going to be frustrated. Just as the car drew up to the crossroads, Mr. Vance spoke up suddenly, "Judith, how about going to see that old plantation I was telling you about?"

"Oh, I'd love to go," Mrs. Vance answered. "How about you two?" She turned and looked at David and Kathy on the back seat.

"Well . . . er . . ." began David.

"No," said Kathy emphatically. "I don't want to go looking at any old house. It's too hot. I'd probably have to keep my shoes on. I can hardly stand having them on; I've been barefoot so long."

Mr. Vance chuckled as he put on the brakes and halted the car. "You've got a point there, Kath," he said. "Tell you what—I guess Mother wouldn't mind getting away from you two for a while. You jump out right here and go on about whatever plot you've hatched up. We'll be back in an hour. And you two be home by four o'clock, or there will be repercussions of a catastrophical nature."

"What does that mean?" asked Kathy.

"It means, be back or else!" threatened Mr. Vance. "Now vamoose, but remember, no swimming. That's a rule. No one is to go into the water without a grown person there too."

"Yes, sir," said David, taking off his clean white shirt and folding it on the back seat. He slipped off his tennis shoes and socks and, wearing only his shorts, he jumped out of the car. Kathy had long since shed her sandals and socks.

"Don't get into any trouble," Mother called as the car started off.

"We won't," Kathy reassured her. David didn't answer. He wasn't so sure.

Of course, Kathy was going to be a problem.

David guessed he couldn't go up to that shack now. It might be dangerous. If only he could think of some way to get rid of her. He might send her off to get the shovel. But he had an idea she wouldn't go. He wished that just once he could have a chance to get out by himself.

"Let's go," Kathy urged.

"Where?" asked David. "We can't go out in the boat. It's gone."

"I know," said Kathy, nodding. "I saw."

"When?" David asked, surprised.

"On the hill this morning," Kathy answered. "You're not the only one who can detect things around here, Mr. Smarty. And what's more I saw some cigarette butts and a dead battery up there. So somebody stayed up there a good while, sending signals."

David chewed his lip. He'd been so busy looking out at the swamp this morning he hadn't thought to look around for clues. But cigarettes and batteries didn't solve the problem of what to do next or how to get rid of Kath.

"Let's go in the swamp along that path where we

saw the pirate," Kathy suggested bravely. "We'll be real quiet, and maybe we can spy on him before he spies on us."

"Listen, Kath," said David, "I hid the shovel in the weeds down the road. About opposite that pier where we went crabbing. Why don't you hop down the road and get it while I stay here and watch for anything suspicious?"

"Why don't you go and let me watch?" Kathy demanded. "You just want to get rid of me, David Vance."

"Well, you can run so fast," offered David. "I thought you'd get back quicker than I would."

Kathy didn't answer; she just looked stubborn, and in the end they both had to go for the shovel. David wished he hadn't said anything about it. He didn't know what they would use the shovel for. There was no map, and there was no boat. He had just about given up hope of locating the place to dig for treasure. But he didn't tell Kathy that.

They found the shovel and turned to go back. "Oh, David, look at the funny chickens," Kathy cried, pointing to the pier.

Two bedraggled, long-legged creatures with big bills stood on the wooden walk. They were covered with damp yellowish fuzz, and their skinny necks were prickly with pinfeathers. As the children watched, each of the forlorn-looking birds took a slow step forward and gazed sadly at the children.

Kathy giggled.

"Those aren't chickens," said David. "Those are some kind of herons or egrets. Young ones whose feathers haven't grown out yet."

"Well, they're funny looking anyway," Kathy answered. "Oh, look! Here comes their momma. And she's all muddy."

The small white egret who landed on the pier beside the young ones did appear to be muddy. Its back was streaked with a pale red-brown color. David, who had seen many of these lovely white birds with spotless plumy feathers wondered how this one had managed to get dirty. "And all the mud around here is black," he thought. "Maybe the storm carried that one way off somewhere and rolled it in some red clay."

He started down the road. Kathy kept turning to

look at the "queer chickens," and they gazed solemnly back. "Come along," David cried impatiently, "we haven't got all the time in the world, Kath."

Kathy hurried to catch up with him. Still carrying the useless shovel, they walked up the road toward Digby until they found the "sort of path" they had followed the day before.

"Now be quiet," David warned. "I mean it, Kath. This may be dangerous."

Kathy looked sulky. "I can be quieter than you,"

she answered. "It isn't me that's always running into things and falling over them."

"That's just indoors," David countered. "Anyway, I mean don't talk. And you know you're the one who's always jabbering."

Kathy opened her mouth to reply and then changed her mind. David turned around and started silently down the path. At least he was silent, but the heavy shovel kept swinging around and hitting branches and tree trunks, and once it hit Kathy on top of her head, and she howled.

David, sweating, lowered the shovel. "I guess there's nobody around," he said in a low voice. "They'd have been sure to hear that."

Kathy rubbed her head. "I wouldn't have yelled if you hadn't whacked me on the head," she pointed out.

"I'm sorry," he said. "Come on."

Twice, water covered the path, which was hard enough to see anyway. Kathy shut her eyes when she waded through the dark water so she wouldn't see the crabs and other creatures who might be after her toes.

David kept looking for something he could recognize. But he hadn't got a very good look yesterday. "It must have been right here we saw the pirate," he said, glancing around.

"I don't see him now," Kathy said. "But I sure smell something fishy. It's awful."

David sniffed. There was indeed an unpleasant odor of dead fish. "Come on," he said. "Let's look around."

128

He dropped the shovel and walked on, looking carefully to the left and right as he went.

"Oh, look at the tree house," squealed Kathy, pointing.

David looked up. Sure enough, on a wooden platform wedged between the limbs of one of the great trees stood a small canvas tent. A rope ladder led up to it.

"Let's go up," suggested Kathy.

David gave her a queer look. He hated to think Kathy was braver than he was. He much preferred to think that she was just too dumb to realize that there might be a pirate sitting up there with a great knife in his hand, ready to plunge it into the first person who stuck his head inside that tent.

"All right," he agreed in a low voice. "But we've got to be careful. Somebody may be up there, waiting for us."

"Oh." Kathy looked apprehensive. "You go first, Dave."

"Well, I certainly intend to," David snorted. He put his foot on the first rung of the ladder and looked up. The tent looked peaceful enough. "But listen, Kath, if anything happens, you run and get help as quick as you can. Mother and Daddy ought to be home by this time."

"Oh, dear," said Kathy. "David, maybe we ought not to go up there."

For answer, David began to mount the rope ladder. He started up spryly enough, but he took very cautiously the rung or two that brought his head up even with the tent.

Slowly he drew aside the flap of the tent. There was no one inside. No one, and nothing. Just the rough wooden floor with its four canvas walls and roof.

"Neat," he commented. "Come on up, Kath."

The little tent just covered the platform. David and Kathy fitted into it nicely, but there wouldn't be much room for anybody else, as Kathy pointed out.

"And there's not room to stretch out," said David. "You couldn't sleep here. I wonder what it's for. And who put it here."

There was a long narrow slit in the side of the tent opposite the entrance. Kathy peered out. "Mother would like it," she remarked. "Look at the birds."

David squinted through the slit. He could see quite a way through the trees because a small pond spread out in front of them. A good many herons and egrets of various kinds stood in the water or perched in the trees.

"Oh, I believe they've got nests," cried Kathy.

Sure enough, several of the herons squatted on big rickety-looking collections of twigs that must be nests. And one or two of the nests had young birds in them.

"That must be what smells so awful," whispered Kathy. "They eat fish, I guess."

David nodded, watching the birds. He could tell snowy egrets, and there were one or two of the much larger American egrets. Some of the dark ones were little blue herons, and some were Louisiana herons. But he'd forgotten which were which. The snowies, a few of which still had their delicate white plumes, seemed to him the most beautiful of all. Two of them shuffled near the tree. He'd never seen them so close. Silently, he and Kathy watched as the two birds gravely waded back and forth around each other, looking for food in the mud.

David had just opened his mouth to tell Kathy

he thought they had better get down, when he heard something. He squatted, still open-mouthed, with his hand on Kathy's arm, listening as hard as he could.

Someone was coming. Someone was walking quietly through the bushes toward the tent in the tree. In the dimness David could see Kathy's eyes grow big with fright. He knew she was thinking the same thing he was. Whoever was coming this way would probably climb up to where they were hidden.

David looked wildly around. If there'd been anything, anything at all, in the tent, he could have
fought with it—at least long enough to let Kathy
escape. But there wasn't a thing. They were trapped.
No one knew where they were; there was no help
for miles around. For the first time David realized
how foolish he had been to say nothing to his father
about all this.

Fearfully the children waited. Now the footsteps
were right under the tent. David even thought he
could feel the limb of the tree shake under the weight
of the intruder. Kathy clutched his hand.

The minutes dragged by. Nothing happened.
There wasn't a sound from beneath them. David
began to feel relieved. Whoever it was had gone on
by, surely.

Moving very carefully, David leaned forward and
raised the flaps of the tent the tiniest bit. At first, he
could see nothing but mud and undergrowth. And
then his eye fell on something long and round and
black. It was a rifle barrel. And the rifle barrel rested
on the shoulder of the pirate, who sat with his back
to a tree trunk, not five yards away.

Chapter 10

Davids's heart thumped hard and fast. He stared at the stern hawklike profile and the round earring dangling above the rifle barrel. Hallucinations, Daddy had said. David only wished this were a hallucination.

Silently he drew back and motioned Kathy to look. And then, silently, they stared at one another. What in the world were they to do? They couldn't even make plans together. The pirate would be on them at once if he heard them talking. Or perhaps he already knew they were there. Perhaps he just meant to sit there, playing a sort of cat-and-mouse game, until the children were forced to reveal their presence.

135

But it wasn't likely. The pirate had walked along as though he hadn't thought anyone was about. And now he seemed to be waiting, as if he was expecting somebody to appear along the path.

Slowly David lowered the tent flap. There was nothing to do but wait. Perhaps the pirate would go away. Perhaps Daddy would come looking for them and scare the pirate away with his shouts. Or they might have to wait till it was dark to escape.

David glanced at his watch. It was almost four. He wondered how long after four it would be before his father started looking for them. And would Mr. Vance think to look in the swamp? Probably not. He would think they were lost in the marsh, because the boat was gone. And there would be at least four more hours of daylight, for even after sunset, twilight hung over the sea and swamp for a good while.

David glanced at Kathy crouching beside him. Her face was white with misery. He tried to grin at her, to show her that, after all, this was just the kind of exciting adventure they were always imagining. But it was a poor attempt at a grin.

The next hour and a half were the most miserable

David had ever spent in his life. The little tent was stiflingly hot, for the canvas walls effectively shut out the air. The smell of the heron rookery was terrible. The children were cramped on the little wooden platform, but they hardly dared move for fear of attracting the pirate's attention. Mosquitoes and gnats hummed in their ears and helped themselves to every inch of bare flesh they could find. David was so thirsty he didn't think he could ever get enough water again.

He looked out at the pirate once more. There he sat, immobile, waiting, just as before. Only once in a while the big earring trembled slightly as he breathed. The insects didn't seem to bother him.

David glanced back at Kathy, and then he knew he had to do something. In another minute she'd be howling. Kathy's face was screwed up tight, and big tears splashed down onto her shirt. He shook her gently by the arm.

"Be quiet," he whispered. "I've got a plan."

But he didn't have a plan. He couldn't think of anything. If only he'd kept his shoes on. Then he might have thrown one into the bushes, and while the pirate was investigating the noise they could escape. But he didn't have anything, not even a belt. His wrist watch, with its plastic band, was so light it wouldn't be heard.

He turned back and studied the pirate as he sat there so watchful and still. And gradually it dawned on David that watchful was not the word. The pirate's head rested against the tree trunk. His eyes were closed, and there was a good chance that he was asleep.

David turned to Kathy and, putting his mouth close to her ear, spoke as loudly as he dared. "He's asleep, I think. Now listen hard, Kath. Stop crying and listen."

Kathy sniffed deeply, took a big breath, and opened her eyes. "I'm listening," she said.

"Well, he's asleep, see," David went on. "So I'll go down first. When I get down, I'll walk a little way over in that direction, away from the path. Then you start down. I'll watch him and if he wakes up, I'll holler and jump up and down and lure him away, see. Then you climb down and run for help. And I mean *run*. You'd better plan on a three-minute mile this time."

Kathy gulped. "But what about you, Dave?" she whispered. "Suppose he catches you?"

"I don't think he will," David answered. "And anyway, even if he does, you run. One of us has got to get away and get help. It's our only chance. And tell Daddy he's got a rifle; tell him to be careful."

"Oh, David, suppose he shoots you," moaned Kathy. "Oh, I'm scared."

"Listen, Kath, do you want to sit up here all night? I don't think he's going to shoot us. We'll just have to take a chance. And remember—as soon as I'm over there by that stump, you start down and *run*," he ordered.

He pushed the tent flap wide and gazed down at the pirate. "He must really be asleep," he thought, "or he'd have looked up."

"I'm going now," he told Kathy, trying to sound calm and brave. But he wasn't feeling brave. He had to turn his back on the pirate to go down the ladder, and it took all his courage. His feet were half-asleep and full of pins and needles. The rope ladder swung and twisted, and he wondered if Kathy would be able to climb down it. She had had a hard enough time getting up. It seemed forever before his feet touched the ground.

When he reached the stump, Kathy was already halfway down the ladder. "It's going to be all right," David thought. "We're going to get away."

He took a step backward on his trembling legs, something gave way under his feet, and with a terrible crash and rattle he fell backward into the bushes.

With a yell, the pirate sprang up. David thrashed

around in the undergrowth trying to get to his feet.

"Run, Kathy, run!" he bawled, scrambling up at last. A hard hand scrabbled at his bare back.

When David fell, the crash made Kathy miss a rung on the ladder and she fell, too. Sprawled on the damp earth, she saw the pirate jump into the bushes

after Dave and heard her brother shout to her. Shaking, she got to her feet and looked wildly around. Was that the path? Was this the way she was supposed to go? She would have cried, only she was too scared to cry.

She flew over the ground, dodging trees and bushes. Once she splashed through water, but this time she didn't worry about crabs. "Is this the way?" she asked herself. "Oh, don't let me get lost. Don't let me get lost."

And then behind her she could hear someone coming through the bushes. The pirate! He hadn't chased David after all. He was chasing her!

The light was dim under the trees, and she couldn't see where she was going. She stumbled over a root and fell to her knees. Panting, she dragged herself up. Not far behind her someone shouted, and she darted off again.

And then just ahead of her a dark figure loomed up among the brush. Kathy skittered into the undergrowth. A briar scratched deep into her arm and tore at her shirt. Her bare feet slipped and slid on the slimy mud. Suddenly she was knee-deep in water with the evil-smelling mire sucking at her toes.

"Quicksand," thought Kathy. "Oh, help!"

Almost anything was better than being buried alive in quicksand. She stood still, trembling and panting. "Help!" she screamed. "Oh, somebody,

142

help!" At least, she tried to scream, but all that came out was a squeak.

But somebody was coming. Somebody pushed through the bushes, and an arm and big hand reached down and hauled her out of the water. Gasping, Kathy looked up into the crimson face and angry blue eyes of the man who had been in the shop with the shark.

"Juan, where are you?" he roared. And then he gave Kathy a shake. "You little rapscallion, what have you done?"

Kathy burst into tears. "Don't kill me!" she sobbed. "Don't kill me! The pirate's already killed David. Please don't kill me!"

Chapter 11

DAVID, who had been bewailing his lack of a shirt all afternoon while the mosquitoes bit him, now thanked his lucky stars that he'd had the good sense to take it off. The pirate's hand raked across his bare back without finding a grip, and with a yelp David sprang away from him.

He rushed through the bushes, fell over a log, and found himself running alongside a boggy pool, until he had to turn away because of a great wall of vines he couldn't get through. Once more he plunged into the undergrowth, clawing his way desperately along.

He planned to make a big circle and come back to

the Digby road as quickly as he could. But vines and bushes and deep pools forced him deeper and deeper into the swamp. Every time he turned toward the road, there was some kind of barrier.

At last he stopped. He stood at the edge of a pool, panting, and leaning against a tree. He felt a stitch in his side, and his legs, already covered with mosquito bites, were scratched and bruised.

It was beginning to get alarmingly dim in the swamp. David was uneasy. He had to get back to the Digby road before it got dark. Once the sun went down, he'd be lost sure enough, in more ways than one.

He thought he heard shouts somewhere off in the distance. Had Kathy got away from the pirate? And how soon would help come? And how would they ever find him? He must get back to the road.

He eyed the pool in front of him. It was black and evil-looking, with a green scum floating on it that reached almost out to the middle of the pond. But if he could get to the other side of it, he might be able to make some progress toward the road. Should he try to swim? His father had said "No swimming," but he hadn't known what the circumstances would be. David put out a foot and touched the green scum. Instantly something rippled away under the surface of the water.

David snatched his foot back and stood trembling. Alligators! This place was probably teeming with alligators!

He stepped back from the pool and began to walk. Maybe he could walk around it. But he'd have to be careful. Even if there weren't any alligators here, there were certainly snakes of every kind, especially rattlers and moccasins.

The pool suddenly widened and spread out before him. Once again the dreadful smell of rotting fish assailed his nose. Around the edges of this shallow lake there must be another rookery of some sort. He'd have to go even farther out of the way to get around this. He turned aside. Right in front of him was a snake. Right on a level with his face, among the branches of a bush, a long black snake dangled. He recoiled with a shout, and the snake suddenly spread great wings and, squealing, flapped away into the dusk.

"Now what was that?" David asked aloud.

He'd have to tell Mother about that bird with its long snaky neck. That is, he would if he ever got home again. The western sky flamed rose and pink. He didn't have much daylight left.

He stood still trying to think what he ought to do. Maybe he ought to try to get back to the marsh. He would run the risk of meeting the pirate, but who knew what risks he was running right here in the swamp? He'd feel better out in the marsh where he had a wider view. Maybe he could wade and swim across the marsh to the causeway.

He turned around and started off toward the sunset. But it was useless. There was more and more water ahead of him. The tide must be rising again. Every little ridge of dry land that he followed ended eventually in a pool or a lake or a stream.

Once he waded across one of these streams, but there was nothing on the other side that seemed to offer better footage. He wished he hadn't done it, for now he was wet and chilly. What was he going to do?

David took off his shorts and wrung some of the water out of them while he tried to calm himself.

147

Just as he got them back on, something in a tangle of vines and young cypresses gave a snort and a grunt and came crashing toward him.

He didn't wait but whipped around and ran, twisting and turning, dodging and pushing, splashing through water, sometimes waist-deep with the muddy bottom pulling at his feet. He didn't have any idea what had come after him, an alligator or a bear or a boa constrictor. But he had no intention of finding out. He meant to get out of there, and quick.

When he finally stopped, he dropped in his tracks, worn out and despairing. It was almost dark, and he was hopelessly lost. He tried not to think of the stories he'd read about people wandering for days in swamps and forests without anything to eat but roots and leaves.

Right now he was more thirsty than hungry, but he knew just how hungry he would be by morning. He could drink the blackish water of the swamp if he had to. But he'd be scared to eat any of the leaves and roots. They all looked poisonous to him.

And maybe he wouldn't live till morning. Maybe some alligator had its wicked eye on him already and was planning to have him for supper right this minute. He glanced around anxiously. And if a snake bit him, he would certainly die before help came, probably before morning.

He might be safer in a tree. But he could never climb one of these big cypresses with their smooth trunks and limbs way up over his head. If he could find a live oak, he might be able to climb that.

David peered this way and that in the shadows. All he could see were cypresses, but over there, where the ground was higher, there might be an oak. In the dim light he set his teeth and waded into the black water. He went steadily ahead. Once he stepped into a hole and had to swim. Something brushed against his foot, and he hoped it was a weed. Shivering all over, he finally dragged himself out of the water and up onto the land.

Yes, there was an oak, he decided. He started forward. A little, dry rattling buzz sounded near his foot, and David froze.

A rattlesnake! He couldn't see a thing. He had no idea where the snake was, or how to avoid it. He tried to keep a grip on himself. It had been a mistake to panic before, and this time it might be

fatal. For a minute his knees sagged with fear, and then with a final angry buzz a big insect flew up and away.

David laughed weakly, but he knew it was no laughing matter. He realized snakes were a constant danger to him, especially now when it was growing so dark. He began to walk slowly and cautiously toward the oak tree. And almost immediately stubbed his toe.

"Oh, ow, darn!" he gulped, grabbing his foot. He was almost crying. Didn't he have enough troubles —wet, cold, hungry, bitten, scratched, and lost— without busting his toe wide open? Whatever had he hit?

He stooped, searching the ground with his hands, and there half-buried in the mud was the treasure.

"It must be," breathed David.

It was a small rectangular metal box with a handle in the lid. The top fitted so tightly that he could hardly feel the crack. It was quite firmly locked; when he pulled on the handle there was no give at all.

"I sure haven't had much luck lately," thought David gloomily. "Here, we've spent so much time and energy trying to find this thing, and now I've found it just when it looks like it isn't going to do me much good."

He picked it up. It was not particularly heavy. "I'll take it with me," he thought. "And then if the pirates, or whoever they are, come after me, I'll throw it in the water somewhere. If I can't have it, they can't have it either, and that's for sure."

He gave it a shake and something inside rattled faintly. What in the world could it be? It certainly wasn't gold. Were rubies heavy? Well, whatever it was, he had it now, in spite of pirates and gangsters.

He walked on toward the tree and found that it was an oak, a huge one. He shoved the metal box into the hollow from which the big limbs spread out. Then he wearily hauled himself up after it. It wasn't very comfortable, and he shoved himself farther up the great branch. A bird flew up out of the leaves crying pitifully, but David was too tired even to be startled. He wondered what kind of a bird it was. He knew a lot about birds now, and he liked them. He wished he'd have a chance to tell his mother that. If he died out here, she'd never know.

He knew the graceful fork-tailed terns and the bigger, more lumbering gulls. He knew the herons and egrets and the brightly patterned turnstones and the dark-fronted, black-bellied plovers. He knew the shy clapper rails, the birds that had made such a racket in the marsh the first time he and Kathy had gone there. And the big half-awkward, half-beautiful pelicans and the magnificent sea ospreys. Now he enjoyed watching them and being able to recognize them. Oh, he'd learned a lot. If he got out of this predicament alive, he would make up to his mother for all the times he'd said mean things about her interest in those little gray-and-yellow warblers.

"And another thing," he thought suddenly. "If I get back alive, I'm not going to go looking for mysteries and treasure and gangsters anymore. When you really get mixed up in something like this, it isn't nearly as much fun as you think it's going to be. And if I see anything suspicious going on, I'm going to tell Daddy."

David yawned. In spite of being wretchedly uncomfortable and more than a little scared, he was tired out. He began to plan what he would do in the morning, but almost immediately he dropped off to sleep.

He woke up to feel himself slipping, and he

grabbed a limb just in time to save himself. He realized then that he couldn't stay in the tree, propped
up on a limb, all night. He'd either have to sleep on
the ground or keep traveling to keep himself awake.
Either choice was dangerous. He shivered, rubbing
his aching muscles, and climbed a little farther out
on the limb. Maybe if he could see some stars, he
might remember something that would help him
get his bearings.

There was something about the Big Dipper. Did
the handle point north? He looked up, but the sky
was still a pale gray, and only a star or two gleamed
in it. But there—there was a big one, low in the
sky. Awfully low, and as he watched, it blinked out
and then on again.

Crossbone Hill! Someone was signaling from
Crossbone Hill!

David grinned. Maybe it was a signal for the
pirates, but it did very well for him too. He watched
and tried to picture the lay of the land in his mind.
Why, why—this tree couldn't be more than a hundred yards from the Digby road. If he went very
carefully in that direction, he ought to find the road
easily.

He scrambled down, seized the box, and headed for the road. He went slowly and carefully, partly because his bruised feet hurt awfully, but mostly

because he was too close to safety now to make any mistakes. He didn't intend to get lost again.

Yes, there was the road ahead of him. He could even see a car coming slowly along it! He hurried forward as best he could, stumbling and falling.

And then right at the edge of the road he drew

155

back. The car was coming closer. It might be Daddy. Or then again it might be a pirate or a gangster or an alligator in a convertible for all he knew. David dropped the box under a bush. In case it was the pirates, he didn't intend to let them have the rubies. But whoever it was, he was too tired to go on any longer. If only it could be Daddy in that car. He stepped out onto the road.

The automobile was only about twenty feet away, creeping along the dirt track very slowly, and the beam of the headlights hit him squarely. The car stopped almost at once and someone jumped out, shouting. A man ran into the beam of light, and David found himself looking into the face of the elderly man with the shark!

Chapter 12

DAVID STARED at the man in a panic. "Run," said a voice in his head. "Run, and get away." But he couldn't run. He was too tired and scared.

And then Mother's voice said, "Oh, David! David, dearest!" And he knew that somehow everything was all right. His knees gave way, and he sagged in a heap on the road.

It was the man with the shark who picked him up and stowed him in the back seat with Mother. David had an idea Kath was on the front seat. He hardly knew what was going on.

Mother said, "What about Phil?"

The shark man said firmly, "We'll get this boy

home and to bed first, and then I'll go get your husband."

Then the next thing David knew he was in a tub of hot water being thoroughly scrubbed with soap and baking soda. He drank something—milk with an egg in it, he supposed, but to him it smelled like a Christmas plum pudding.

When he opened his eyes again it was daylight, and Kathy was sitting on the edge of his bed. He stared at her and she burst out laughing. She laughed till she fell off the bed.

"What's so funny, Miss Smart Alec?" he asked indignantly.

"Wait, wait," she gasped, and got up and brought a small square mirror off the wall.

When he saw himself, he grinned a little. His eyes were swollen almost shut. The worst of his insect bites had been dabbed with something white, so that he looked like a clown. There was a big red scratch down one cheek and a big blue bruise on the other. In between he was dotted with freckles and bites.

"I guess I do look kind of funny," he admitted. "But you look sort of measly yourself, Kath."

Kathy took the mirror and regarded herself gravely. She was pretty well-bitten and scratched too. "I don't look as gruesome as you do," she said finally.

David threw a pillow at her.

"Here, here, what's going on?" asked Mr. Vance from the doorway. "You must be feeling pretty good, Dave, or is fighting with Kathy such an ingrained reaction you'd do it no matter what?"

"I'm fine," said David. "Except my legs are sore." He stuck them out from under the covers and howled in horror. His legs were awful looking. His feet and ankles were puffed up to twice their normal size, and there was hardly any skin left on them. "Gee," he said finally, "I wish the guys at school could see me now."

Mr. Vance chuckled. "The honorable scars of war. Judith! Dr. Lavender! Come see the wounded hero, and then let's get to the bottom of all this."

Mrs. Vance and the man who had had the shark and who was evidently Dr. Lavender—although David still thought of him as the gangster—came in and inspected David's bites and scratches.

"A prize collection," commented Dr. Lavender.

Mother brought David's breakfast on a tray and

while he ate, Daddy arranged chairs for the three adults in the tiny room. Kathy crouched at the foot of the bed.

"Now, David, we haven't had a word of explanation about all this," said Mr. Vance. "Last night Kathy was incoherent, and this morning we decided we wouldn't ask her anything until you were awake and could help her keep a firm grip on the truth."

David swallowed his orange juice and nodded. He could hardly bring himself to look at Dr. Lavender. He still didn't know who the doctor was, but it was quite evident he wasn't a gangster, or even an ex-gangster.

"Now, Kathy, will you please tell the story? And, David, will you kindly let us know when her imagination causes her to stray too far from the facts?" Mr. Vance continued. "All right now, Kathy, on your mark, get set, go. And, David, crunch your toast as quietly as possible.

Kathy drew a deep breath while David spread lots of raspberry jam on his toast to make it as noiseless as he could. "Well," she began, "it started with Crossbone Hill. You know, Daddy, you said yourself there were pirates around here. And I just knew

160

they'd buried treasure somewhere. So David and I went into the marsh, and on the edge of the swamp we found a bird's nest. And it had a map in it."

David gulped down his scrambled eggs and added, "Not just lying in it, but woven into the nest, the way birds do sometimes."

"A wood thrush's nest, probably," murmured Dr. Lavender. "They always like a piece of paper woven into the walls."

"Anyway, it was a map of Crossbone Hill and the marsh and the swamp," Kathy went on. "And it showed a cross mark for buried treasure with 'pirate rubies' written beside it."

David looked up from his third piece of toast. "Not 'pirate rubies,'" he corrected. "'Pira' and a squiggle and 'rub' and a squiggle."

"Well, it looked like 'pirate rubies' to *me*," said Kathy. "So we tried to mark the spot at the edge of the swamp. And then we met him—"she nodded toward Dr. Lavender—"with his hammerhead shark, and he said, 'Stay out of the swamp if you value your life'"—Dr. Lavender chuckled—"so we knew he was hot on the trail of the treasure."

Kathy paused and drew another deep breath.

162

"And that night we saw somebody on Crossbone Hill signaling with a light to someone in the swamp," Kathy went on. "So next morning we tried to go into the swamp from the Digby road. We went in and I guess we must have found the spot where the treasure is hidden, because the place was full of horrible pirates, and they chased us, and I guess they would have made us walk the plank if they'd caught us, but they didn't."

David drained his milk glass and set it down carefully. "Oh, Kath, you are a bubble brain. There was only one pirate, and he didn't chase us. He just yelled at us to get out."

"We only saw one," pointed out Kathy. "But the woods were probably full of them. And then it stormed. And yesterday morning Daddy took us up on Crossbone Hill. There was a dead flashlight battery up there. And the boat was gone."

"The boat?" asked Mr. Vance. "What boat?"

"Our boat, that goes with the house," David told him. "So you see, Daddy, we thought someone was trying every way possible to keep us out of the swamp. I tried to leave Kath out of this, Daddy. I tried to sneak off without her, but then you and

Mother dumped us out on the road, and she wouldn't stay behind."

"Well, I should say not," Kathy exclaimed. "So we went into the swamp, Daddy, and we came to this horrid-smelling place, and there was a tree house with a rope ladder. And we got up in the tree house, and there was just room for us, so we started to come down, and there was that mean old pirate waiting for us with his gun. We had to stay up there for *hours,* and it was hot, and we didn't have room to move around, and things bit us, and . . ." She paused for breath.

"So when I noticed the pirate was asleep," David took up the tale quickly, "we sneaked down the ladder. Only I fell over something and woke him up. I ran off with him after me, and I got away, but I couldn't find my way back to the road. There was so much water, and I was afraid of snakes—and alligators," he added.

"David was brave," said Kathy. "He did everything first, and he tried to save me from the pirates, and I reckon he did."

"I wasn't very brave," David admitted. "I was plenty scared when it got dark and I was out there in the swamp. But I climbed a tree and I saw the lights on Crossbone Hill, so I knew where I was then, and I got back to the road, and you all found me."

David and Kathy looked at Daddy.

"I congratulate you on telling a perfectly logical and lucid story, not one word of which I can understand," said Mr. Vance. "What is all this about treasure and pirates?"

Dr. Lavender cleared his throat. "I think I can clear up most of this mystery," he said. "And I'm exceedingly sorry for my part in it. Although I sincerely doubt," he added, looking at Kathy thoughtfully, "if any explanation I might have offered could deter a young lady with such singularly involved mental processes."

David grinned. "That means you're a bubble brain, Kath," he said, and ducked as she made a swipe at him.

"My name is Robert Lavender," said the elderly man. "I am a retired professor of political science, and I live at my family home, the plantation called Lavender Blue which is about five miles from here. At one time my grandfather owned most of the land around here and I still own a good part of the marsh and swamp, including the section with that deserted shack on it."

"Oh, I forgot about the smoke coming from the shack," spoke up David. "And I forgot about Mother's blue bird-book disappearing too."

"Well, the shack isn't deserted at all," went on the professor. "That's a fable which I encourage. I use it often. In fact, I've been living there almost all the time since the first of March.

"You see, for a great many years political science has interested me less and less, and the natural world has intrigued me more and more. I didn't need the salary attached to my professorship, so as soon as I could, I left my position and came home to devote my whole life to the study of birds and trees and flowers and fish and all the other wonderful and beautiful creatures who live in this part of the world. I'm especially interested in birds," he added, and he smiled at Mrs. Vance.

"And I thought he was a gangster," David said to himself.

"At Lavender Blue I have a respectable family and several servants, but out here in the swamp I have only Juan," Dr. Lavender continued. "Juan is my old friend and companion. He's a Spaniard, and he doesn't speak much English though he's been with me for years. He looks after me as best he can, cooks and sweeps out the shack, and helps me out in many ways. For instance, as you may know, it is always helpful to have someone accompany you into a bird blind. The birds see you go in, and they are uneasy and watchful. But if someone leaves, the birds are relieved. They don't notice that only half as many people leave as went in. They only know someone came and someone went away, so they go about their business as usual, which is what the observer wants."

"I guess that tree house was really a bird blind," hazarded David.

Dr. Lavender nodded. "Yes, I have been watching that heron rookery since March. But to get back to Juan. He is rather fierce looking, and he will wear that ring in his ear, but this is the first time he's been mistaken for a pirate. He's my right-hand man. Among other things that he does for me is to retrieve the books and papers that I am apt to leave lying about when I get interested in something else and forget about them. No doubt that's what happened to your mother's bird guide. If Juan found a book on the beach, especially one about birds, I'm afraid he would assume it was mine and take it home without looking to find out. It's probably among my books right now."

"Oh, gee, Mom, I sure am glad," breathed David. And Mrs. Vance smiled at him.

"Juan must have slipped up once in picking up after me," continued Dr. Lavender. "For I'm almost certain that Kathy's treasure map was a rough map, locating some birds' nests in the swamp, that I made several years ago. I think the pirate rubies were actually a summer tanager's nest. The tanager's Latin name is *Piranga rubra,* and the squiggles are a sort of shorthand I use."

"Oh, dear," sighed Kathy, "rubies are my birthstone."

"What about the lights on the hill?" asked David. "And why did the pir—why did Juan—have a rifle?"

"Oh, the lights are another of Juan's duties," Dr. Lavender answered. "You see, as I said before, I'm absent-minded and what's more, my sense of direction is not too good. Sometimes I go into the marsh or the swamp in a boat at night, and then Juan stands on the hill and shows a light every now and then to guide me home. For the swamp is an easy place to get lost in, even in daylight, and even when you are as familiar with it as I am."

"Well, why did he do it last night?" David wanted to know.

"To guide me," answered Mr. Vance. "When we discovered you were in the swamp I took the boat, which Juan had had the good sense to pull up onto high ground when he saw the storm coming, and I went looking for you. Fortunately, before I had a chance to get lost myself, Juan gave me the signal that meant you'd been found."

"We were on the way to Digby to get help in the search when we saw you," said Mother. "Dr. Lavender hoped you would see the light and perhaps find your way back to the road by it."

"And to get back to the rifle," said Dr. Lavender. "I'm afraid it was a piece of disobedience on Juan's part. He knows I dislike having him shoot in the swamp. It disturbs the birds and makes them shy. But Juan loves possum better than anything, even

169

me. He knew that there would be eggs and nestlings on the ground at the rookery after the storm, and that possums would probably come looking for these delicacies. So he took the rifle with him to get himself a treat for supper."

"So I guess that takes care of all the mystery," said Mrs. Vance cheerfully.

"Yes," answered David. "All except . . ." He stopped and dropped his eyes, a little embarrassed.

Dr. Lavender smiled. "All except why Juan and I were so anxious to keep you out of the swamp," he said. Suddenly he looked rather sad. "Well, you see, there's more to my story, and it doesn't have a very happy ending for me. There *was* a treasure in the swamp after all. It all began in Africa!"

Africa! David sat up straighter. This ought to be interesting. He glanced at Kathy, and he could tell right away that she was thinking of carved ivory idols and tigers and voodoo goddesses, and goodness knows what else. It was just like Kath to think there were tigers in Africa.

"In Africa, in parts of Asia too, and even in Spain, there is a small white heron called the cattle egret.

It is a beautiful bird with a fondness for the insects stirred up by the movement of herds of cattle through grass and bushes. About twenty-five years ago, these little egrets appeared in South America. Apparently they had been blown across the Atlantic from the Old World to the New.

"They settled down happily in their new territory and increased rapidly. Most ornithologists were exceedingly provoked to think that such a tremendous happening as the arrival of a whole new species on a new continent hadn't been more scientifically noted and observed. The birds were well established before anyone seems to have noticed them."

He stopped and nodded his head.

"Well, of course, there are more trained observers in North America than in South America, and the country's more accessible. When the first cattle egrets landed in Florida and Texas, I guess you might say that ornithologists rolled out the red carpet for them. All over the country bird-watchers were on the alert, and these egrets were seen as far north as Massachusetts, even Canada. And when they first nested in Texas, you can be sure the bird-watchers' world knew all about it." He looked at Mrs. Vance. "I presume you already know all this?" he asked, and she nodded.

"Well, this spring was the first spring in my life when I had no duties or responsibilities or engagements of any sort, and I meant to devote every minute of it to the birds in the swamp and the marsh. I came over here about the first of March and got things running smoothly.

"My blind by the rookery was all built and ready, and I had books and photographic equipment in plenty. I was looking forward to this adventure very much. The snowies started nesting unusually early, and everything was going according to plan when one day I noticed that one pair of snowies weren't snowy egrets at all. They had reddish plumes on head and back such as I had never seen before.

"They were cattle egrets. And a nesting pair was something every bird-watcher would want to see." He stopped and scratched his jaw self-consciously.

"I'm a selfish old man. I'd planned things very well. I didn't want a lot of strangers tramping through my swamp, frightening every nesting bird, getting into my hair and under my feet. And I was afraid too. It has happened before that people coming to see some rarity like this have scared it away."

He shook his head and looked apologetically at Mrs. Vance.

"You see it was the first time the cattle egrets had nested this far north. It was bound to create a lot of interest and stir. I decided to say nothing about it. I wasn't going to have my spring spoiled. I wanted to keep a complete record of the egrets' nesting, and I intended to keep everybody out of the swamp— everybody. Of course, very few people ever think of going into my swamp. There aren't even many hunters around here anymore, and the swamp doesn't appeal to most people. So it gave me quite a shock to find that two venturesome youngsters had moved in so close to the rookery.

"And then everything began to go wrong. First, a colleague of mine who had suddenly become ill asked me if I would fill a speaking engagement for him. Well, I owed him a lot, so I agreed. My young egrets were half-grown, and I had almost a complete record on film of the mating and nesting and brood-rearing of these rare birds.

"I left Juan with instructions to keep you youngsters away from the rookery if he could, and he certainly tried. And then, while I was gone, the storm came. The whole bush in which my egrets were nesting disappeared, and so have the birds."

"Do they look like snowies with red clay on their backs?" asked David suddenly.

The professor looked surprised. "Why, yes, they do," he agreed.

"Then they're on our crabbing pier," said David. "At least they were yesterday. Kathy found them. She thought they were some kind of funny-looking chickens."

"Well, bless my soul!" exclaimed Dr. Lavender, and then once again he looked sad.

"But the real treasure for me, of course, was the film, most of which was in color. I had it in a metal box. I meant to have it developed by a friend of mine who specializes in doing just that sort of thing.

"I took the box out to the rookery with me just before I left, and I removed the last films from my cameras. Juan and I brought the cameras back to the shack, but in my typical absent-minded fashion I set the box down and went off and left it. I didn't think of it again till I was on the train. Of course, there was no way to get in touch with Juan immediately, but I didn't worry about it. I thought it would be safe, for the box was locked and quite weathertight. Even if it rained, the film would be safe. But when I got back, I couldn't find it. The high tide must have swept it away. I suppose it's in the bottom of the swamp now."

David moved his sore legs under the blankets. So the treasure was only a roll of film. What a disappointment! And he'd planned on being rich!

"No, it isn't," he announced gloomily. "I know where the box is, too."

Chapter 13

"I NEVER SPENT so much time on a vacation sitting around waiting to get well," grumbled David. "First we got our feet sunburned, and now this! Can't I ever go swimming again?"

His mother eyed him speculatively. It was the day after the explanation of the mystery, and all the Vances were suffering a letdown. Yesterday David had been content to lie in bed and let his bruises heal. But today he was bored and restless.

The morning had been long, lunch had been dull —Vienna sausages again—and the afternoon stretched ahead of him. It looked monotonous indeed

176

in spite of the fact that Daddy had just come home announcing that he couldn't work.

"I worried about what kind of mix-up you were concocting now," he said. "I think I'll stay home a few days and establish some kind of order in this household."

Now Mother said slowly to David, "Well, I suppose there's nothing against your swimming this afternoon. Not that I think you'll enjoy it particularly."

"Oh, boy!" cried David. "Let me get into my trunks." And then he stopped. "What do you mean, I won't enjoy it?"

Mrs. Vance smiled. "Oh, you'll see what I mean. And as soon as Daddy's ready, we'll go in."

David went outside and tried to help Kathy corner a tiny sand-colored crab which sidled over the sand faster than thought.

"Gee," said David, "you'd think six legs would get in your way. But they sure seem to be a help to him. I guess it's all in knowing how to use them."

"Think what he could do on roller skates," said Kathy, laughing and pushing her feet through the hot loose sand so that it squeaked.

"Come on, you two," called Mr. Vance. "I'm ready to brave the billows. You bloodhounds get your sheriff's badges, and let's go."

"Oh, Daddy, we aren't going to try to solve any more mysteries, honest," giggled Kathy.

But within minutes David solved a mystery of his own. He plunged into the cool waves with a shout of joy, and then immediately let out a howl. At first he thought a jellyfish had him, for he stung and burned all over. It was the salt water getting into all the bites and scratches and raw places on his skin. So that was what Mother had meant! "Wow!" he thought. "I can't stand this. I'll have to get out."

But he gritted his teeth and bore the stinging for a few minutes longer, and surprisingly it stopped. He swam for a while, but his muscles were still sore. At the end of half an hour he was glad to come out onto the beach. He took Mother's field glasses and watched some sandpipers while the others finished their swim.

As they walked back to the house Kathy cried, "Oh, look, someone's coming to see us!"

And sure enough a car was rattling along the road. It was a very ancient car, and it shook and wheezed on the rough road. It stopped beside the Vance's house, and Dr. Lavender got out.

"Daddy," whispered Kathy, I thought you said Dr. Lavender was rich."

"Oh, yes, he's quite well-off," said Daddy.

"Then why does he drive that old car?" demanded Kathy.

"I think Dr. Lavender is one of the really sensible people of this world," said Daddy. "He sees no reason to part with something simply because it is old and perhaps out of fashion. He likes his car; it still runs well; so he keeps it."

Dr. Lavender, dressed in rough, worn clothes, was sitting in the living room waiting for them when they trooped into the house. "I came to invite you to dinner at Lavender Blue tomorrow night," he said, getting up. "And to tie up the tag ends of the mystery."

He had, it seemed, located the cattle egrets on the pier where they had caught the crabs. "The whole bush, with the nest and family still intact, must have been swept up against the pier," he told them. "The mother made a valiant attempt to hold her family together, but the change of environment was too much for her. So I've made arrangements for the conservation station to take over their care. And who knows, maybe next year we'll have several pairs nesting here."

He pointed a finger at David. "And thanks to you, Juan and I located my box of film, unharmed, and it's gone off to be developed. So everything has turned out better than I could have hoped."

"Well, that's wonderful," said Mrs. Vance. "And we do apologize for any trouble we've caused you."

"Not at all," said Dr. Lavender. "I was the one who caused the trouble. As a matter of fact, I have here a little memento." He reached in his pocket. "This is to make up for having raised your hopes of having riches and then so unduly dashing them."

He held something out to Kathy and she took it. It was a tiny circlet of gold leaves enclosing another circle of small pearls, with a little red stone in the center.

"A ruby," whispered Kathy. "A real ruby."

"Yes," Dr. Lavender said, nodding. "Rubies were my mother's birthstone, and the little pin was hers. She was an imaginative young lady too, and I know she would have liked you to have it."

"Oh, how beautiful!" gasped Kathy.

At the same time Mother said, "Oh, but Dr. Lavender, isn't it too . . . well . . . er . . . valuable?"

Dr. Lavender looked gravely at the pin. "In view of the infinitesimal nature of the ruby, I would say no," he announced judiciously. "Its value lies only in its ability to remind Kathy how few pirates there are left in the world."

Kathy turned scarlet, and David looked out the window. The old pin was all very well, but he certainly didn't care anything about it. And after all he was the one who had found the box of film.

"And as for David," Dr. Lavender continued, "I hope you have no objection to letting him accept the reward I was prepared to offer for my box of film. I had already written out an ad to post in the Digby store, offering fifty dollars for its return."

Fifty dollars! David's eyes bulged. He was ashamed of the way he'd felt a minute before. He looked at Mother and Daddy, and they looked at him.

"I . . . I'd . . . better not take it, Dr. Lavender," he mumbled. "I . . . I just stumbled on the box. It was just a lucky break."

181

"Nonsense," said Dr. Lavender. "The cost of the film alone was more than that, and its value to me beyond measure. This is truly the reward I was offering, and I want you to take it."

"Go ahead, Dave," urged Mr. Vance. "I think Dr. Lavender really wants you to have it. And I hope whatever you buy with it will serve to remind you that your father isn't such an old fuddy-duddy that he can't enjoy a little mystery too if you're willing to share it with him. And sometimes it saves such mishaps as getting lost in the swamp."

"Gosh, Daddy," said Dave. "I did try to tell you once. But it sounded too corny."

Everybody laughed, and David took the check from Dr. Lavender with polite thanks. He stood, staring at it. His English racer was right here in his hands, almost. Or maybe he'd be sensible and keep his old bike, the way Dr. Lavender still kept his old car. After all, the old bike was still good. Then David grinned to himself. He wasn't sensible, and he knew it. He meant to have that racer just as soon as he got home.

Dr. Lavender got up to leave. "Oh, by the way, a friend of mine has asked me to come to his plantation day after tomorrow to see his white ibises. He's got quite a rookery. Would you like to come?"

"Oh, I'd love to," Mrs. Vance cried. "How about you, Phil?"

"Not me, thanks," Mr. Vance answered. "I'm going to stay home and lie in the sun and recuperate from all this excitement."

"Me too," chirped Kathy. "I know a good place on the beach where treasure might be buried. I'm going to stay here and dig."

Dr. Lavender laughed. "All right. How about you, David? There's plenty of room in the boat."

David didn't hesitate. He'd seen pictures of white ibises, big storklike birds with red faces and great curved red bills. He'd give anything to see one in person. And maybe there would be another of the snaky-necked anhingas which had frightened him in the swamp, too.

"Sure, count me in," he replied. He grinned at his mother, and she smiled back.

"We're very lucky, you know," Dr. Lavender went on. "As a rule, this friend does everything he can to keep people away. Says he doesn't want people tramping through his swamp. He's a regular old miser with his birds. I can't understand it." And he gave Dave a big wink and went out.

David stood looking after him. Dr. Lavender was a great guy. But, he, David, was a lucky boy. He'd only been at the beach a week and look what had happened to him already. An exciting mystery, a new and wonderful hobby, and the money for an English racer. And most of the long sunny days of an ocean vacation still lay ahead of him.

In spite of his still-sore muscles, he couldn't keep still. He ran across the porch, slamming the screen door behind him, and flung himself down on the hot soft sand.

"Great Jolly Roger!" he shouted. "Hurray for Crossbone Hill!"

ABOUT THE AUTHOR

WILSON GAGE is the pen name of Mary Q. Steele, the newest writer in a family of gifted and successful writers; her husband, William, her sister, and her mother, Christine Govan, are the authors of many popular books for children and young people. With her family's penchant for storytelling it was inevitable that Wilson Gage should try her hand at writing. Her first book *Secret of the Indian Mound* quickly established her in the children's-book field.

Wilson Gage is a graduate of the University of Chattanooga where she received a bachelor's degree in physics and mathematics. "I was married before I was out of college," she says, "and have been washing dishes quite steadily ever since. I love the outdoors, but in an unathletic way. I just like to walk around and smell the flowers and watch the birds." She now lives at Signal Mountain, Tennessee, with her husband and their three children.